6/22

Rainbows, Rowan and True, True Romance(?)

"Hope you have a great few days!" Mum smiled, self-consciously stepping towards her own mother, as if she didn't know whether she deserved to join in the general hug-a-thon too.

"Thank you, Melanie, dear," Grandma beamed, clasping Mum close, but letting her go again quickly. It was funny; I almost got the feeling that Grandma was on the verge of getting emotional, but trying to cover it up with her usual no-nonsense, no-fuss approach. "Now we're back on Saturday. You *will* still be here, won't you, Melanie?"

From the smile on Grandma's face, that last remark was supposed to be a joke. Or was it? Was it Grandma's way of asking Mum what her plans were without panicking any of us? (Except that now, little old worrier me was *already* panicking.)

"Me? ...Of *course* I'll still be here!" Mum laughed in reply.

Pity she hesitated for that split-second before she spoke, though...

Available in this series:

The Past, the Present and the Loud, Loud Girl
Dates, Double Dates and Big, Big Trouble
Butterflies, Bullies and Bad, Bad Habits
Friends, Freak-Outs and Very Secret Secrets
Boys, Brothers and Jelly-Belly Dancing
Sisters, Super-Creeps and Slushy, Gushy Love Songs
Parties, Predicaments and Undercover Pets
Tattoos, Telltales and Terrible, Terrible Twins
Angels, Arguments and a Furry Merry Christmas
Mates, Mysteries and Pretty Weird Weirdness
Daisy, Dad and the Huge, Small Surprise

And look out for:

Visitors, Vanishings and Va-Va-Va Voom
Crushes, Cliques and the Cool School Trip
Hassles, Heart-pings! and Sad, Happy Endings

Find out more about Ally's World at
www.karenmccombie.com

RAINBOWS, ROWAN AND TRUE, TRUE ROMANCE(?)

KAREN McCOMBIE

SCHOLASTIC

For Miss barbara tHomson,
MRS christine McIntyre
and MR NORMAN constable.
(Hey, teachers <u>can</u> be cool!)

Scholastic Children's Books,
Commonwealth House, 1–19 New Oxford Street,
London WC1A 1NU, UK
A division of Scholastic Ltd
London ~ New York ~ Toronto ~ Sydney ~ Auckland
Mexico City ~ New Delhi ~ Hong Kong

First published in the UK by Scholastic Ltd, 2003

Copyright © Karen McCombie, 2003
Cover illustration copyright © Spike Gerrell, 2003

ISBN 0 439 98203 0

Typeset by TW Typesetting, Midsomer Norton, Somerset
Printed and bound in Great Britain by Cox & Wyman Ltd, Reading, Berkshire

10 9 8 7 6 5 4 3 2 1

Contents

PROLOGUE

Dear Mum,

I know you're here at the moment (well, you're in Sainsbury's right now, strictly speaking), and that I can tell you stuff in person (i.e. once you get back from Sainsbury's), but the thing is, while you were away, I kind of got into the habit of writing down everything that happened to our family and my friends, and I think I'd really miss doing that. So if it's OK with you, I'm going to keep scribbling all our sagas – even if you *are* here to see them – and then when I'm done, you can make a cup of tea, pull up a cat and read all about us.

Anyway, apart from realizing that I didn't want to stop writing my journals, I learnt two things today: first, black olives make our dopey dog Rolf barf (mind you, he *did* eat the entire bag you left on the kitchen table this morning – including the *actual* bag).

The second (and more important) thing I learnt was that while I am an expert in the art of worrying,

I'd much rather be that than shy. Wondering what I'm waffling on about? Well, it's like this; as you know, Sandie is one of my best friends. Absolutely. A hundred per cent. Cross my heart and hope to die. But there *are* moments when your best friends can send you loopy, and that's exactly what Sandie – the reigning holder of the World's Shyest Person title – did to me this morning. I know being shy isn't much of a crime, like being a carjacker or a money launderer or a pirate or something, but then if Sandie *was* a carjacker or a money launderer or a pirate, she wouldn't show me (or herself) up so horribly.

Here's what happened: we were in HMV, and Sandie was being served by the most gorgeous, aloof, sulky teenage boy in the universe. After ogling him, we scarpered outside, only to find that Mr Aloof had short-changed Sandie big-time. But would she go back in and tell him he owed her another fiver? Of *course* not – she was way, way, *way* too mortifyingly shy to do that, no matter *how* much I tried to convince her that she couldn't let herself be ripped off, even if it *was* by accident.

Can you guess what happened next? Yep ... after much begging from Sandie, *I* – complete with a tomato-red face and an attractive stammer – ended up trying to explain to Mr Aloof about the mistake with her change. He stood listening, chewing gum and acting like I was about as interesting as constipation, while Sandie hid behind a display of Enrique Iglesias CDs. (Couldn't she at least have chosen something cooler?)

Then Mr Aloof asked to see her receipt, but even though I was waving at her like a demented windmill, Sandie refused to come out from behind the CD display. So muggins me had to go and get the receipt off her, *then* walk the walk of shame *back* to the counter with it while Mr Aloof and his fellow aloof sales blokes got the sniggers at me and my dumb mate. Who by this time, incidentally, was doing an impersonation of a startled meerkat as she peeped over the top of Enrique's CDs. Very cool. *Not*...

I guess that means we'll never dare shop in that particular branch of HMV ever again, all thanks to Sandie's shyness making us both look like a right pair of turnips.

Ah, well... I won't hold it against Sandie (even though I can *still* hear those boys snickering as we slouched out), 'cause even *I'm* not immune to the occasional dollop of dumb, tongue-tying shyness myself, as you'll soon see, Mum...

Love you lots,
Ally
(your Love Child No. 3)

PS Sorry if talking about barfing, shyness, constipation, meerkats and turnips all at once is a bit confusing, but, er, that's just me! (Better get used to it...)

MY AMAZING SHRINKING VOICE

"Hmmm … miniminimmm…"

It was a teeny-tiny sound, and came from quite a small, pink thing. The sound was some kind of happy, tuneless hum, and the small thing was called Ivy, who happened to be my sister (something I *still* hadn't quite got my head around yet). The pinkness was the colour of her clothes, from her shorts to her T-shirt to her size "titchy" plastic sandals.

"Ppppttt-*uhhh*!"

That was *another* teeny-tiny sound, and came from an even *smaller* thing. A small *furry* thing this time.

"What was that?" I asked, staring down at the sleepy-looking gerbil that Ivy was gently holding and humming to, and wondering if I'd just heard my first ever gerbil fart.

"A sneeze," my brother Tor informed me as he scrubbed away at the bottom of the cleared-out cage with a bottle of disinfectant and some wildly over-sized yellow rubber gloves. The ends of the empty fingers were squidging and wibbling around like they were made of lemon jelly. From her curled-up position on the dusty shed floor, our dog Winslet – pretending she was asleep – watched the wibbly-ended gloves with interest with her one opened eye. I guessed that the minute Tor took the gloves off, Winslet would nab them to add to one of her many strange doggy treasure troves hidden in the deep, dark depths of our house.

But back to the second teeny-tiny sound: of *course* the "Ppppttt-*uhhh*" noise was a *sneeze*. After all, that was the whole reason I was spending a sunny Monday afternoon stuck inside the garden shed with a seven-year-old boy, a very small girl, a sneaky dog and a germ-ridden rodent. I was sure there were more exciting things to do on the last day of the summer holidays (for example, Rowan was currently stretched out on a rug in the garden, trying to turn herself into a tanned goddess for the new term), but I really didn't mind helping Tor spruce up the shed-cum-sickbay. Apart from anything else, it was a perfect opportunity to get to know Ivy better. She may have been on the planet for three-and-a-half years, but all of us had only known her since Saturday afternoon, when Mum arrived out of the blue with her, so I guess you could say there was a bit of catching up to do.

"Do you think…" I muttered, leaning in close to peer at the gerbil nestling in Ivy's arms, "…that Pickle would like a diddy little hankie for his diddy little snotty nose?"

I was just goofing around for Ivy's sake, but instead of smiling, she stopped her humming and crinkled her nose in confusion. So far she'd hardly said a word, and hardly smiled either. Mum told us that was just Ivy … a chip off Tor's silent block. Though weirdly, Tor had been a whole lot less silent in the last couple of days since Ivy'd shown up. He'd really taken a shine to her, specially once he realized she was just as much of an animal nut as him. Don't get me wrong; it wasn't as if he'd exactly turned into a motormouth or anything, but it seemed that being around a kid even quieter than himself had somehow stimulated Tor's vocal chords. Or maybe it was just the excitement of having Mum around that had got him in the mood for yakking. Funnily enough, it was having the opposite effect on me…

"*Branston*," said Tor, taking his lemon jelly fingers out of the cage and grabbing a handful of fresh, straw-type bedding out of the plastic sack next to him.

"Branston? What are you on about?" I asked, now that it was my turn to be confused.

"It's my gerbil's name, Ally!" Tor corrected me, looking aghast at the fact that I could have got such an obvious thing wrong. "Not *Pickle*."

Ivy nodded hard. Ah … so *that* was what had got her crinkling her nose at me just now, and not just my useless attempt to goof around. Maybe I was coming across as a bit of a failure in her big, brown eyes. Urgh … the *last* thing I wanted to be was a disappointment of a big sister *already*.

"I knew it was Branston! I was only joking!" I lied with a big grin. "I *know* there's not a Pickle!"

"Yes there is!" Tor corrected me again. "He's Branston's brother!"

"Um … I knew that too! I was just being silly…" I tried to cover up, knowing that Tor and Ivy didn't buy my excuse for a *second*.

"Ppppttt-*uhhh*!" Branston sneezed again, sending millions of minuscule particles of bacteria shooting off around the shed.

I was about to ask out loud if it was possible for humans to catch gerbil germs (I didn't fancy "Ppppttt-*uhhh*!", "Ppppttt-*uhhh*!", "Ppppttt-*uhhh*!"-ing my way through assembly tomorrow morning), when I realized that Tor would take it as a terrible slur against his sickly pet, and I was in enough trouble with my little brother as it was. Nope… I needed to steer the subject away from gerbils and on to something else. Something that would make Ivy realize that in my own way, I was just as cool as Tor.

"OK, OK!" I burst out. "How about I tell you both a story?"

I settled on story-telling, as the only other things I was good at were worrying, eating crisps and beating the rest of my family to the shower in the morning, and I didn't suppose any of that would particularly impress a three-and-a-half year old. (Although Ivy *might* have been quite amazed at how many tortilla chips I could cram in my mouth at once...)

"What story?" Tor asked, delicately lifting Branston out of Ivy's arms and depositing him and his gerbil germs inside the newly renovated cage.

I hadn't a clue. I'd been so desperate to change the subject that I'd said the first thing that came into my mind. But under Ivy's intense gaze, I knew I'd have to come up with something smartish, or risk disappointing my brand new kid sister for a second time.

"Right..." I nodded, hoping that the nodding might shake an idea out of my brain cells somehow.

Two eager faces stared expectantly at me. Make that three; Winslet had opened *both* her eyes now, although I had a sneaking suspicion that while Tor and Ivy were waiting for a story to trip off my tongue, Winslet would have preferred to hear the magic words, "Teatime!" Well, tough cookies, hairy dog – teatime was a long way off.

"Um … once … once upon a time…" I wiffled, hoping for a thunderbolt of an idea.

And then it came; inspiration washed all over me like a warm bath. (OK – it wasn't quite as poetic as that; it was more of a small *ping!* in my head.)

"Once upon a time," I began again, with a bit more assurance in my voice, "there lived a boy and a girl, called Martin and Melanie."

Tor beamed, immediately recognizing the start of this story. Ivy continued to stare intently at me with her huge brown eyes, waiting to hear what was going to happen next. Winslet just disappointedly flopped her head back down on the floor and started snoring loudly, since I hadn't mentioned anything remotely related to food.

"The girl – was she beautiful?" Tor asked, as familiar with this fairy tale as he was with our family. Which wasn't surprising, because it wasn't so much of a fairy tale as the tale of our family, and I'd told it to him a couple of zillions of times before, on those occasions when nightmares had sent him scurrying to the sanctuary of my bed.

"Yes, she was beautiful," I nodded.

"And was the boy kind and funny?"

I thought of the photos we had of our dad when he was young and smiley and scruffily cute.

"Yes, Tor, he was kind and funny. Anyway, the boy and the girl met—"

"In a bike shop!" Tor interrupted.

"Yes – they met in a bike shop where the boy worked, and they fell madly in love over the spare tyres."

Tor giggled, but Ivy didn't. Guess it was going to take her a while to tune into my lame-brain sense of humour.

"And because they were in love, they got married, and became Mr and Mrs Love, 'cause that was their last name. Then they had Love child number one, who was called…"

"Linnhe!" Tor yelled out, making Ivy jump.

"*Then* they had Love child number two, who was called…"

"Rowan!"

"Yep!" I laughed. "*Then* they had Love child number three, who was called…"

"Ally!"

Ivy widened her eyes at the mention of my name, and muttered "Ally!", which made me go a bit wibbly, actually, 'cause just about all I'd heard her say up till then was "Ben!" (the name of her dog back home in Cornwall) and "Yum!" (It seemed our Ivy wasn't a fussy eater and liked her food – although she hadn't tried Rowan's cooking yet...)

"*Then* they had Love child number four," I continued, knowing this was Tor's favourite bit, "who was called..."

"Tor!" yelped Tor.

"Tor!" repeated Ivy softly, looking like she was starting to enjoy this game.

"And *then* they had Love child number *five*, and *she* was called..."

This was a new addition to the story. Neither Tor or me said anything; we both just leant forward, grinning at Ivy and wondering if she'd get it. Just as she glanced wordlessly between us, another voice altogether gave the right answer...

"Ivy!" Mum called, as she stood in the shed doorway, her hands on her hips and her blondie-brown, wavy hair backlit like a halo by the sun. "Looks like you're all having fun!"

As she spoke, Ivy went running towards her, and wrapped her arms round Mum's long denim skirt (and, of course, the legs underneath it).

"Ally was telling us a story!" Tor explained, since I'd magically managed to lose my voice.

"So I heard!" Mum laughed, stepping inside to

join us. (Not easy when you have a small child attached to your legs.)

Eek! I thought in a panic. *How long has Mum been standing there listening in?*

I knew there wasn't any real reason to be embarrassed about the idea of her earwigging on the story I'd been telling, but *you* try explaining that to my stupid cheeks, which were flushing as pink as Ivy's T-shirt right at that second.

"Anyway," she smiled, gently untangling herself from Ivy's grasp and settling herself down on the shed floor, cross-legged. "What have you all been up to while I've been away?"

Wow. *That* was a difficult question to sum up quickly. Me and Linn and Rowan and Tor had all grown up, I guess. Apart from that, we'd made loads of new friends ... accidentally started up an animal sanctuary in the house for wonky, unloved pets ... and Linn had got bossier ... Rowan had got ditzier ... Tor'd turned into a mini-Rolf Harris (minus the beard)...

Oops! As Mum smiled enquiringly at me, I suddenly realized that she meant what had we been up to *this afternoon* while she'd been round at Dad's bike shop keeping him company. She had *not* meant what had we been doing for the last four years while she'd been gone.

Doh…

Mum was still smiling at me, still waiting for an answer, looking just as beautiful as I imagined her in the fun-size fairy tale I'd just told Tor and Ivy. And the strangest thing was happening; I *might* have wanted to answer her, and I *desperately* wanted to ask her how she and Dad were getting along and if they'd sorted everything out between them, but as my grandma would say (and she likes her sensible sayings), you can't always have what you want. It was bizarre; even as I tried to form the words in my throat, I could physically feel my voice *shrinking*, for goodness' sake…

"Aaarkk!"

Mum, frowned a little at the strange squawk that had squeaked out of my dry-as-a-desert mouth. This was terrible: Linn was taller, prettier and smarter than when Mum had seen her last; Rowan was more of a creative, interesting airhead; and me? Mum was probably staring at me and thinking, "I don't remember having a daughter as demented as *this* one!"

Good grief, what was wrong with me? Shouldn't I have been starting to *relax* more in her company, instead of feeling as shy as a five year old on her first day at school?

"All right, Ally? Got a tickle in your throat or

something?" Mum checked with me, looking all concerned.

Got a screw loose in my head, more like, I groaned to myself, as my voice still refused to crank up.

Thank goodness there was someone more idiotic than me on hand to drag Mum's attention away from my predicament.

"Rowan?" Mum asked quizzically, as a human tornado in flip-flops and a Union Jack bikini appeared panting at the shed door.

With her rows of multi-coloured metal bracelets jangling, Rowan held up a crumpled magazine, and jabbed her finger against it till it rustled.

"I... I... I..." she jabbered, jumping up and down on the spot and making no sense at all. Not that anyone would have been able to hear her – all that frenzied jumping and rustling and jangling had woken Winslet from a deep sleep and set her off barking for Britain.

"*What?*" I shouted at Rowan, finding my voice at last, as I risked life and limb by attempting to clamp Winslet's jaws together.

"I... I'm... I'm *famous*!" Rowan finally blurted out, before promptly bursting into tears.

Oh, good grief. Now Mum would think she had *two* demented daughters. I wouldn't have blamed her if she'd flung all of Ivy's pink clothes in a suitcase and taken the first train back to Cornwall...

Chapter 2

RONAN LOVE – SUPERMODEL!

"Look! It's even got my name underneath!" Rowan giggled.

"'*Ronan*'," stated Tor.

"Huh?" I muttered, then saw what Tor was getting at. Under the smiling full-length snap of our sister, a sentence read: "*Sussed for summer, Ronan Love (aged 15).*"

"It's close enough," shrugged Rowan, unfazed by the magazine's boo-boo.

"But Ronan's a *boy*'s name!" Tor answered indignantly. "*You're* not a boy!"

Well spotted, Tor. Rowan – the most glitter-obsessed girlie girl in the universe – could *never* be mistaken for a boy.

"I don't mind," Rowan sighed happily. "Not now they've made me famous!"

Yikes. We practically had our own Kate Moss in the family. Yes, Rowan – sorry, *Ronan* – Love was a star. Nearly. Well, it's not *every* day you look in a trendy style magazine and see your sister staring back at you…

But thanks to Branston the sickly gerbil, we didn't immediately get a chance to figure out why Rowan had become famous. As soon as my sobbing sister had shuffled into the shed and ceremonially opened the magazine she was carrying, Branston ruined the moment by stretching his neck through the bars of the cage and nibbling on page ninety-three. (Well, your appetite is always a bit funny when you're ill, isn't it?)

Rowan squealed in horror when she saw the nibbling going on – you'd think she'd spotted Branston tucking into a twenty pound note the way she flipped. And so – still stumped about what was going on – we'd all had to relocate from the shed to the sanctity of the kitchen before we could discover the mysterious wondrousness of Rowan's fame. Ivy, however, seemed to have lost interest; while we were all huddled around the kitchen table gawping at the article Rowan was featured in, she'd pulled a chair over to the wall and clambered up on it, and was now covering a photo of a Golden Retriever pinned on the message board with trillions of tiny kisses.

"You look wonderful, Rowan!" said Mum, as she leant on me and Ro's shoulders and gazed down at the magazine.

What she *meant* was, Rowan looked amazing in the photo in front of us. You couldn't really have described her as looking amazing in her *current* outfit, unless you wanted to describe it as amazingly *weird*. Over the top of her Union Jack bikini, she was wearing the brown and beige gingham apron that Grandma usually slung on when she was doing the housework. To be fair to Rowan, it wasn't exactly a style statement on her part – it was the first thing she'd laid her hands on when Linn had barked at her to cover herself up and put some clothes on.

"I love the butterflies," Mum cooed, lifting her arm from around my shoulders and pointing at the photo.

"Futterbies!" came a small girlie voice from over by the wall.

The butterflies (or "futterbies", if you happened to be three and a half) were made of felt, and Rowan had sewn them up the leg of her jeans, to match her favourite T-shirt – the one with the butterfly logo on it. She also had a floppy felt butterfly nestling in her hair, stitched on to an old hairclip.

"Where was this taken?" asked Mum.

"Portobello Market!" Ro replied. "I was there with Von and Chazza. I didn't know it was for a magazine at the time – this photographer just came up and asked if he could take a photo of me for a project he was doing about cool stuff that real people wear!"

"Don't you mean, 'fashion mistakes that real people make'?" teased Linn as she clanked a bunch of glasses and a carton of orange juice down on the table for everyone.

"That's not very nice to say to your sister, Linn!" said Mum, sounding surprised, and shooting Linn a strange smiley frown (or was it a frowny smile?).

Linn stopped smirking straight away, as if she'd been slapped. Oops – it didn't look like Mum understood that Linn and Rowan sniping at each other is as normal round here as three-legged cats sleeping on top of the fridge (and if you know our house, you'll know that's normal). And it didn't look as if Linn appreciated being told off by Mum, even in the smiliest of ways...

"It must have been three months ago that it happened," Rowan ruminated to herself, oblivious to the slight edge of an atmosphere that had sprung up in the room. "Wonder why it took that long for the photo to get printed in here?"

"It's called lead-time," said Alfie knowledgeably.

Oh, yes – we were in the presence of my boyfriend Alfie (i.e. my boyfriend in a parallel universe). Alfie was the one who'd bought the magazine, spotted Rowan's picture in it, then rushed round here to show us all, bumping into his best mate Linn on the way. Of course, Alfie's presence was the reason Linn had so grouchily requested Rowan to cover up. And Ro's resulting strange bikini 'n' apron combination was the reason Alfie was gawping at her right now. After all, although even he was used to her dressing pretty madly, today Rowan really *did* look as if she was about to be arrested by the fashion police at any second.

"What's lead-time?" asked Tor, his attention grabbed by the word "lead". (Honestly, anything remotely linked to animals and his radar ears prick up.)

"It's the length of time magazines need to get all their pages together, and to get printed and stuff..." Alfie explained, shrugging his skinny, muscly shoulders in his effortlessly cool T-shirt.

Sigh...

"Ooh, look at the time!" Mum gasped all of a sudden, checking the face of her watch, just as a cat that wasn't Colin bounded up on the table and started settling itself down for a snooze on the magazine. "I'll have to start thinking about what to make for tea!"

Wow. Mum announcing she was making something for tea. I hadn't heard her say that for about … four years.

"Tea? But it's way too early!" Linn jumped in, her hand freezing in mid-air as she poured out glasses of orange juice.

"Still, it won't be long till your dad's home from work," Mum answered cheerfully as she turned away from the table and padded over to the fridge, examining the contents.

"Yeah, but when he comes home, he likes to have a shower and catch up with us first. We don't eat straight away!"

Oh dear. "Tetchy", that's how Linn sounded to me. I didn't know if Mum had picked up on that (she was still studying what was lurking in the fridge), but the rest of my family certainly hadn't: Rowan was too busy pulling the magazine out from under Fluffy's bum, Tor was too busy patting Fluffy, and Ivy was still kissing the picture of her dog back in Cornwall. Then I wondered if maybe Alfie had sussed the tetchiness in the air, seeing as he was such a good mate of Linn's, but he was still too traumatized by the state of Rowan to pay any attention to the ongoing tea conversation.

"Well, there's no harm in me just looking things

out," Mum chattered easily, with her back still to us, while pulling open the vegetable tray at the bottom of the fridge.

"There's no point," said Linn tartly. "I've got it all organized. It's *my* turn to make tea."

"Your turn?" Mum queried, still smiling but looking confused as she turned around.

"We have a rota," Linn said brusquely. "Grandma normally makes us tea during the week, and us girls and Dad take turns cooking the rest of the time. That's the way it's worked since…"

Linn's words hung in the air, but they might as well have been propped on the roof of the house in two-metre-high neon letters, they were so obvious.

"…*since you left us*…" I practically heard Linn yell telepathically at our mum.

Mum's pretty sensitive. *She* knew. I could tell that from the way she looked so flustered, passing the limp lettuce she was holding from one hand to the other, as she tried to come up with something to say.

And then a friendly "*coo-eee!*" broke the strange mood that only Linn and Mum and me seemed to be aware of.

"Hello, everyone." Grandma smiled around the room as she and Stanley breezed though the hall and into the kitchen. Her eyes hovered for a second on Rowan and her bizarre outfit, but she knew our airhead sister well enough not to ask useless questions like "Why...?" when it came to her choice of clothes.

"Aaargghh!" roared Stanley, scooping up Ivy from the chair she was perched on and making her giggle with his bear hug.

"Our cab's outside," Grandma explained, dodging to the left as Tor bolted past her to join in the roaring, tickling, bear hugging going on behind her. "We just thought we'd pop in for a second and say goodbye before we left for the station."

Yep, by the time we were all heading for bed tonight, Grandma and Stanley would be gazing out of their hotel-room window at the delights of Edinburgh. Five days in Scotland maybe wouldn't be *everyone's* idea of a glam honeymoon, but then I couldn't really see my grandma and Stanley paragliding off the back of a speedboat in the Maldives either.

"Can me and Ivy go round and play with Mushu while you're away?" Tor asked in a wibbly-wobbly voice, as Stanley held him by the waist, upside down.

"No, sweetheart – I told you, Mushu's staying with our neighbour."

Tor had taken it as a personal snub when

Grandma decided against checking Mushu into the Love Pet Hotel for the few days they were in Scotland. But I think Grandma was worried that her perfect Siamese kitten might pick up some bad habits (not to mention fleas) from our mangy lot.

"Have a lovely time, Grandma!" Linn suddenly burst out, coming around the table for a hug.

"We will," said Grandma, stepping over to give me and Ro a two-at-a-time hug once Linn had let her go.

"Hope you have a great few days!" Mum smiled, self-consciously stepping towards her own mother, as if she didn't know whether she deserved to join in the general hug-a-thon too.

"Thank you, Melanie, dear," Grandma beamed, clasping Mum close, but letting her go again quickly. It was funny; I almost got the feeling that Grandma was on the verge of getting emotional, but trying to cover it up with her usual no-nonsense, no-fuss approach. "Now we're back on Saturday. You *will* still be here, won't you, Melanie?"

From the smile on Grandma's face, that last remark was supposed to be a joke. Or was it? Was it Grandma's way of asking Mum what her plans were without panicking any of us? (Except that now, little old worrier me was *already* panicking.)

"Me? ...Of *course* I'll still be here!" Mum laughed in reply.

Pity she hesitated for that split-second before she spoke, though...

Chapter 3

THE CONVERSATION THAT WENT "CLUNK"...

It's easy to keep me happy.

Having an ordinary, run-of-the-mill meal can make me delirious with joy. How come? When my long-lost mum (and surprise new sister) are sitting at the same table as me, *that's* how come.

And call me shallow ("Ally, you're shallow"), but one small "bye" will keep me smiling like a goon for hours. If it's said by Alfie, of course. "Bye, Ally"; those were his exact words. Two simple but wonderful words that made me practically throw up with happiness when Linn saw him to the door not long ago.

Oh, *when will he see sense and realize that a thirteen-year-old scruff-bucket like me with boring hair and no chest to speak of is his dream date?!?* I mused to myself as everyone settled down around the much-more-squashed-for-room-than-normal kitchen table.

"Ally – pass the salt," said Rowan, interrupting my happy meanderings.

She'd changed out of her bikini and apron, I noticed, and into her "street style" butterfly-adorned outfit.

"Sure, there you go, *Ronan*," I grinned, sliding the salt cellar across the table towards her.

Ro stuck out her tongue at me good-naturedly as she bent over to scramble for the salt cellar that had zoomed past her outstretched hand and clattered on to the floor. (Funny that she never got picked for the netball/basketball/rounders teams at school...)

"See? It's *you*!" I heard Tor say, and turned to see him pushing a side plate over towards Ivy, showing off to her the outline of a girl he'd made from a long strand of cooked spaghetti.

"Yum..." Ivy mumbled, studying it for a second before picking it up and sucking it all in in one go. Luckily, Tor was too impressed by that to take offence at her eating his artwork.

"Yum – exactly!" Dad nodded in Ivy's direction. "This bolognese is great, Linn!"

"Thanks, Dad." Linn smiled across the table at him. "Nadia's mum's bolognese is always really nice, and she puts tonnes of oregano in it, so I bought some today, specially."

"Who's Nadia?" Mum asked brightly, as she leant sideways and tried to tuck a sheet of kitchen roll into the collar of Ivy's pink T-shirt. (Too late – the pink was already splattered with splodges of tomato sauce.)

"Just a friend. You don't know her," Linn replied bluntly, addressing her answer to her plate. "So, Dad – how're you getting on with that order of bikes for that lawyer bloke and his family?"

Dad looked momentarily flummoxed. I could tell that he wasn't flummoxed about the order, but that one of us kids was actually *interested* in it. I mean, we all love Dad dearly, but you could hardly blame us for nodding off when he starts blabbing on about spokes and ten-speed camshafts or whatever. The fact that Linn was asking him about it – well, that was just plain bamboozling to him.

"What order's this then?" Mum asked.

"It's a really important order – it's worth a lot of money, isn't it, Dad?"

You'd think Mum was a ventriloquist who'd thrown her voice. I mean, why else would Linn look at Dad when she was answering Mum's question?

If you want to know the truth, I was starting to feel a little sick, and it wasn't down to the food. (Hey, it's not like it was Rowan's turn to make tea.) It was because of Linn – what was she up to?

It wouldn't have been too far off the mark to say she was verging on being plain *rude* to Mum. Did anyone else notice? It didn't seem so, after a quick glance around the table.

God, I hope Linn stops that, I thought to myself, winding spaghetti round and round on my fork and forgetting to eat it. *We need Mum to feel, well* ... welcome, *or she might not want to stick around...*

"Tell us more about the craft shop you work in, Mum!" asked Rowan, as she reached across for a hunk of bread.

Good old Rowan. She might not have realized it, but she'd changed the subject at *just* the right time.

"Well ... let's see," said Mum, tucking some wisps of wavy hair behind her ear. "It's very sweet. It's smaller than your dad's shop, but it has the same set-up, with a studio out the back. We all take turns working on our stuff, but mostly it's me or my friend Val who serve out front, because Liam is always too messy, what with doing all the pottery work. He looks like the abominable cement man sometimes, he's so covered in caked-on clay!"

Me and Rowan and Tor all sniggered at that, and it was lovely to see Mum laughing too. Ivy didn't join in; she was too busy feeding spaghetti to something under the table. Linn and Dad … well, they didn't seem to be doing much smiling at all.

"Um, this Liam… Who's he exactly?" Dad asked tentatively.

Urgh – it sounded as if Dad was asking if "Liam" was her *boyfriend*, for goodness' sake. But maybe that was just me picking it up wrong.

"Like I said, he works in the shop and in the craft studio with me and Val. He makes pots," Mum replied almost coolly, her laugh slip-sliding away.

Yikes. So it *wasn't* just me. Looked like Mum thought she was being cross-examined too.

"Tor's been doing lots of arty crafty stuff this summer, haven't you, Tor?" Linn burst in.

OK, so I took it all back about Linn. She *didn't* deliberately want to go upsetting Mum *after* all – here she was, steering the conversation away from any awkwardness.

Tor nodded enthusiastically but in true Tor style didn't bother to add any more to Linn's statement. Still, he'd just stuck a whole meatball in his mouth, so maybe talking (make that *choking*) would have been dangerous to his health.

"Oh, that's lovely, Tor!" Mum enthused. "You'll have to show me what you've been up to! Did Grandma or your sisters help you?"

"No. 'Aizzee," Tor mumbled through his mouthful of meatball.

"He means *Daisy*," Linn clarified.

"Daisy?"

Mum's fair eyebrows arched on her smooth, lightly suntanned forehead as she spoke.

"She ran the summer club Tor went to," Linn explained breezily. "And she was Dad's *friend*."

Good grief, Linn couldn't have heaped more meaning into the word "friend" if she'd had a shovel. From the way she'd said it, it made it sound as if Daisy was practically living round here and asking us to call her "mom". And I'm sure, from the flushed expression on her face, that that was the way Mum picked it up.

Hey, what a fun, family meal *this* was turning out to be – I *don't* think...

I really miss my old alarm clock.

OK, so it didn't keep time, but what's twenty minutes (slow or fast, depending on its mood) between friends? I was gutted when it finally gave up telling even the *wrong* time and stopped altogether. And I should have been grateful when Grandma bought me this nice, shiny new alarm clock. But me and it, we just weren't getting along. For a start, it was boring and predictable (where's the fun when you can't make bets with yourself about what the time *really* is?). Then there was the alarm part itself; it was like being wakened by a large man clattering metal dustbin lids against either side of your head every morning. And as for the ticking ... even now, even though it was in the bottom of my wardrobe wrapped up in my thick towelling dressing gown, I could *still* hear it tick-tock-ticking away like a strange form of torture.

I was lying awake, knowing it was very late, but toying with the idea of getting up and burying the stupid clock in the garden, when my bedroom door quietly squeaked open. I expected it to be one of four things:

a) a dog (either Rolf- or Winslet-flavoured)

b) Colin

c) a cat that wasn't Colin

d) Tor, with a soft toy or five in tow.

What I got instead was a ghost. At least, that's what I thought it was at first. What do you expect when you see a white-faced figure in a floaty Victorian-style cotton nightie wisp their way into a room? This *was* the attic, after all, the place where young servant girls would have slept when the house was first built a hundred or so years ago. So was this the ghost of some fifteen-year-old chambermaid, come to ask me what I was doing in her bed? Or to see if I fancied swapping for a day, with me eating lukewarm porridge for breakfast and polishing the fireplaces, while *she* ate peanut-butter sandwiches and watched *Home and Away*?

With my heart pounding, I squinted hard and saw that it *was* indeed a fifteen-year-old girl, but no Victorian ghost would be wearing trainer socks with Lisa Simpson on them.

"What have you got those on for?" I whispered to Rowan, nodding at her feet as I switched on my bedside light.

"I thought I heard one of the cats barfing on the landing, and I didn't want to risk stepping in cat puke in the dark in my bare feet," she whispered back, gathering up the folds of her white cotton nightie and settling herself cross-legged on my bed.

"Fair enough. So what's up? Couldn't sleep?"

"Nope." She shook her head, her dark curls bobbing round her face as she spoke. "So … first day back at school tomorrow!"

"Yep. I'm sort of looking forward to it in a weird way," I replied. "What about you?"

"Yeah, kind of," Ro shrugged.

"Are you going to take the magazine in? Show everyone what a superstar 'Ronan' Love is?" I teased her.

"No – I *don't* think so!" Rowan giggled self-consciously, but she couldn't fool me – I'd already spotted her putting it in her schoolbag earlier in the evening.

Then I shut up for a second, to give Ro a chance to tell me what had brought her scurrying up to my room in the middle of the night. It had to have something to do with Mum being back, didn't it?

"Want to see the stupid thing I did?" she grinned sheepishly.

"Go on, then."

Rowan tended to do quite a lot of stupid things, and they were always entertaining.

"Look!" she giggled, hauling up her nightdress. At first I thought I was supposed to be looking at her purple-striped knickers (and wondered why she'd think I'd want a close-up nosey at them) but then I saw what she was *actually* on about – a great big white handprint on her pinkly tanned tummy.

"I fell asleep for a while this afternoon when I was sunbathing – must have slept with my hand across my stomach!" she sniggered.

"Honestly, Ro, you *are* a complete dingbat," I grinned back at her, as she hauled her nightie back down.

Then we fell silent again, both smiling at Rowan's general goofiness.

"Ivy's cute, isn't she?" Ro piped up.

But you know, somehow, I didn't think Rowan had risked stepping in cat puke just to come up here and show me the handprint on her tummy or chat to me about how cute Ivy was. Although she was. Cute, I mean. But I was totally wide awake anyway, so I didn't particularly feel like hurrying Rowan to get to the point.

"Do you think Tor thinks she's a pet?" Rowan asked.

"Probably," I nodded, thinking back to the vet programme him and Ivy were glued to before bath and bedtime. Ivy had sat curled at Tor's feet, while he'd distractedly patted her head. At one point I'd even thought Ivy was purring, but no, it was just a cat that wasn't Colin, fast asleep under a vibrating copy of Dad's *Mountain Biking UK* magazine.

"Yeah..." Rowan muttered vaguely, while playing with the white ribbon at the neck of her voluminous nightie.

Silence for a couple more seconds. And then Ro finally got it off her chest.

"Ally, what was Linn playing at today?" she burst out suddenly, making me spin my head around to check she'd closed the door behind her. (She had.)

The last thing we needed was to wake the Grouch Queen herself and have her come through to tell us to shut it, in no uncertain terms.

"She *was* pretty bad," I agreed, quite stunned to realize that I wasn't the only Love child who'd noticed our big sister's barbed comments earlier.

"*Bad?*" squeaked Rowan. "She might as well just buy Mum and Ivy two tickets back to Cornwall and get it over with!"

"I know…"

"Why all of a sudden is she trying to drive Mum away, Ally? I mean, at first, she seemed as pleased as we were to have her back!"

"I don't know," I shrugged, totally stumped. OK, so Linn had bristled a bit when Mum told her off for being mean to Ro, but the stirring she was doing tonight during tea didn't help matters between Mum and Dad one little bit.

"And it wasn't just Linn! When we were all sitting around the table … the way Mum and Dad were talking to each other … it was so … *clunky*!" Rowan sighed, slapping her hands across her face.

"I know," I agreed with her again, thinking that "clunky" was the perfect way to describe the awkward, stilted conversation between our parents (made all the clunkier by Linn with those digs about Daisy etc.).

"Oh, Ally…" sighed Ro, opening her fingers wide enough for me to see the worry in her eyes. "It *is* going to be all right, isn't it? Mum *is* going to stay, isn't she?"

"Of course!" I reassured Rowan, folding back the duvet so she could snuggle in beside me. "Mum and Dad just need a bit of time to get things sorted, that's all."

"Yeah? Do you really think so?" I heard Rowan ask, as I flicked the light out and plunged the room into darkness.

"Sure!" I answered in my brightest, breeziest voice.

Lucky it was so dark, or Rowan might have spotted the telltale quiver I always get at the corner of my mouth when I'm lying…

Chapter 4

"BABY BEAR" AND BARFING

"So let me get this straight," said Chloe, fixing her eyes on mine. "Your mum went backpacking for a few months, ended up staying away for four years, let your whole family believe that she was travelling the world, but all the time she was just in *Cornwall*?"

I nodded. It was bizarre but true.

"And the *reason* she didn't get any further than Cornwall was 'cause she found out she was expecting a *baby*. I mean, she was already pregnant when she set off, but didn't realize it at the time?"

"Right," I nodded again.

"But she never came home, or called your dad to explain or anything because…"

"…because she was suffering from a kind of depression thing, only she didn't know it." I filled in the blanks, totally aware that it was a lot to take in (my brain had practically *melted* the last few days, trying to get it straight in my head). "And even once she got better, she didn't get in touch 'cause she thought she'd mucked everything up with us; that maybe she'd left it too long and we'd all be better off without her."

"Wow…" Chloe muttered. "Finding all that out must have been just so … *wow*!"

The rest of my friends hadn't been quite as stunned as Chloe when we got together for our first breaktime chat of the new term. That's 'cause Sandie and Kyra had already phoned around Kellie, Salma and Jen and filled them in on my shock news. But Chloe had been over in Ireland for the weekend, visiting relatives. All *she* thought she was going to be hearing about was my grandma's wedding. She thought I'd be yakking about terrible wedding outfits and embarrassing speeches and badly behaved little kids and maybe the odd so-called "adult" throwing terrible drunken dance moves at the reception. It's safe to say that she hadn't expected to hear me announce that my mum had finally turned up after all this time, with a mystery little sister in tow too. Mind you, *I* hadn't exactly expected to hear myself make an announcement like that either.

"So, what does she look like now?" Chloe asked, her ginger (sorry, *auburn*) eyebrows furrowing into a frown.

"Exactly the same as I remember her," I shrugged,

feeling flutterings of happiness and – stupidly – *shyness* again as I thought of Mum's smiling face when she'd handed me a bowl of cornflakes this morning.

"Anyway, all the time Ally's mum's been away, she's sent home photos of herself, so Ally's *always* known what she looked like! *Duuuh!*" Kyra pointed out, in her usual charming way (i.e. she stuck her tongue behind her lower lip and pulled a face at Chloe).

Chloe, blanking Kyra completely, continued quizzing me.

"And so what's your little sister *like?*"

"*Sooooo* cute! Isn't she, Al?" Sandie burst in. "She'll only dress in pink, won't she? And she looks *exactly* like Tor, only she's a girl, of course!"

"Wow…"

Chloe's head slowly bobbed back and forth, like an old-fashioned nodding dog toy.

I knew how she felt. My head was still reeling so much from the events of the past few days that I'd daydreamed my way right through our extra-long, welcome-back assembly, and only realized it was over when Kyra nudged me in the ribs with her sharp, pointy elbow, and told me to "Move it, doughball!"

"Little Ivy from St Ives…" Kellie sighed, her

dark brown eyes glistening with the excitement of it all. "It's so weird to think that none of you knew Ivy existed, not even your dad!"

"Tell me about it!" I laughed wryly.

"But can you imagine how weird it is for Ivy?" said Sandie. "Suddenly having a dad and a brother and a whole heap of sisters all at once?"

Hey, that was a good point. I'd never even *considered* how baffling it must be to arrive in the Love household and find that all us mad people in there – never mind the zoo's-worth of pets – are your new family. And you know something? Funny, quiet, serious little Ivy seemed to be taking it all in her small stride.

She was one cool kid...

"'Cause if it was me, I think I'd be really freaked – oh! Hold on!"

Sandie stopped in the middle of what she was saying and rummaged around in her blazer pocket for her polka-dot pink mobile.

"Hello? Oh, *hiiiiii*!"

In a nano-second, Sandie turned into The Amazing Jelly Woman, visibly wibbling and wobbling at the very sound of the voice chattering in her ear.

Billy.

It had to be.

No one else could turn Sandie to mush as

quickly as that. Good grief; on the way to school this morning, she'd already told me that her and Billy had spent the whole of yesterday together. And now here he was, phoning her up at morning break, like he couldn't wait to talk to her. *Boy*, those two had it bad...

"Do you? *Really*? Ooh, and I miss you *too*!" she cooed into the mouthpiece, instantly oblivious to the rest of us. "No – I miss you *more*, Baby Bear...! No – I *do*, I miss you *more*... Hee, hee, hee! No – miss you *more*!"

"Baby Bear"?! Sandie actually called Billy "Baby Bear"?! *Bleurghhhhh*...

"Oh, *please*!" Kyra muttered blackly, narrowing her eyes in Sandie's direction. "I think I'm going to barf!"

Chloe, Kellie and Salma snickered at that, knowing exactly what she meant.

"No, Kyra – *I* want to barf *more* than *you*!" I joked at Sandie's expense, even if she *was* too distracted with love-sickness and her "Baby Bear" to notice.

It wasn't so much the fact that Sandie and my oldest, *bestest* boy mate were going out that bothered me, it was just the way they talked and acted so slushy-gushy towards each other that made me feel squeamish.

"Oh, leave her alone!" Jen grinned. "I think it's totally *sweet*, the way they talk to each other."

"Oh, go on, Billy! *You* say it. No – *you* say it first. No – *you* say it!" Sandie giggled into the phone, swaying back and forth on one leg as if she was a very laid-back tightrope walker.

"Oi, where are you going?" Salma said loudly, as Kyra started sloping away from us, heading around the corner of the building we were all leaning against.

"Shhh!" Kyra responded, holding one finger against her wickedly grinning face, while scrabbling around in her bag.

"What's she up to?" Chloe hissed at me, as if I might psychically have a clue what was going on in Kyra's twisted mind.

"*I* don't know!" I shrugged, while Sandie continued to twitter lovey-doveyness over the phone in Billy's direction.

"Why do you all give her a hard time about it? Wouldn't you like to be in love like her and Billy?" Jen chastised us all. "I know *I* would!"

"I'd rather be single for ever or stick a sharp pencil in my eye than be caught talking all that mushy stuff with a boy!" Chloe growled low, smirking at the sight of love-struck Sandie.

"No, you would *not*! I bet when *you* fall in love with someone—"

But Jen didn't get a chance to finish her defence; we all jumped when Sandie let out a surprised yelp and jerked the phone away from her ear as though it had sent a two zillion volt shock directly into her eardrum.

"What's wrong?" I asked, rushing over. I may have the occasional small laugh at my friend's expense (doesn't everyone?), but if something *was* seriously the matter, then I'd be the first one in there to help her out...

"I – I – I'm not sure!" Sandie cried out, holding her phone out towards me.

I grabbed it and clamped it to my ear, and was practically deafened by the noise. Somewhere in the muddled roaring, I could hear Billy yelping, "Gerroff! Leave me alone, you morons!", while a cacophony of male voices cackled and made kissy-kissy noises.

"I *wuv* you, *Sandieeee*!" someone bellowed into the phone so loud their voice was distorted. But not distorted enough for me not to recognize it. And all of a sudden I twigged ... even as Kyra came swanning back towards us, shuffling her phone back into her bag, I *knew*.

"Sod off, Richie!" I shouted back down the line, with a grin, before cutting off the connection on Sandie's phone.

"What? What's going on?" asked poor, confused Sandie, unaware that Kyra had pulled the best practical joke on her and Billy. Y'see, Kyra used to go out with Billy's mate Richie/Ricardo (the name's a long story, and I use the term "mate" loosely, since Richie/Ricardo is a total drongo), and I guessed she still had his mobile number keyed into her phone's address book. So it didn't take too much effort for her to call up Richie/Ricardo, tell him to look out for Billy (they go to the same school), and then for Richie/Drongo/Ricardo and Billy's other buddies to pounce on him when he was in mid slushy-gushy mode.

It was mean, but it was funny – it really was. I couldn't help laughing, alongside Kyra, and Chloe and Kellie and Salma and Jen, once Kyra explained to them what she'd done.

But when I looked at Sandie's crestfallen face, and watched her try to be a good sport and smile through her confusion and embarrassment, I felt like a good friend *minus* a thousand.

After all, back home, the one thing I was wishing for with *all* my heart was for romance to blossom again between Mum and Dad. So how could I be horrible and take the mickey out of Sandie being all loved-up?

If I was a proper, true friend, I should be happy

for her. And from now on I would be. (Only please don't let her call him "Baby Bear" in front of me ever again, or I really *would* barf...)

Chapter 5

SEAWEED SOUP...

"Ooh! That's ... that's *lovely*, Ivy!" I smiled, trying to let the panic subside.

Normally, I come home for lunch instead of staying for school dinners because my nice calm home is like an oasis in the middle of the day. Not that it's *that* calm, with the dogs and cats and things squeaking and squawking up in Tor's room, never mind the blast of some Aussie soap as Rowan settles herself down in front of the telly with a ham and jam sandwich, or whatever disgusting concoction she's come up with.

Today would be different, I knew, since Mum and Ivy would be at home, but I still jumped when I opened the front door and found myself immediately pounced on by a small girl and two frantically barking dogs.

"Ben! BEN!" yelped Ivy, holding a piece of paper up under my nose with both her pudgy little hands.

"Oh, so it is!" I humoured her, as I studied the

big, blue splodge of crayon in the middle of the slightly crushed sheet of paper.

I wriggled out of my blazer and tried to shush Rolf and Winslet, who seemed plain delirious to have someone around to play with all day. (Usually when I come home at lunchtime, they're both sprawled hairily somewhere, tongues lolling, dreaming doggy dreams of sausages and tree-sniffing.)

"We're through here, Ally!" I heard Mum call out as she appeared in the kitchen doorway like a hippy mirage. She was wearing a long, patterned cheesecloth Indian skirt (which had hung in the wardrobe gathering dust for the last four years) and a rust-red T-shirt with one of her own designs on it (which *might* have been a seagull, or maybe it was a whale, or maybe even a kite or something – it was kind of hard to tell).

"Will we go through and get some lunch?" I asked Ivy, as the smell of some herby, home-made soup wafted through and tickled at my nostrils.

"Yum!" said Ivy in reply, before racing off with the dogs towards the kitchen.

"So how was your first morning back?"

That was Mum's question, but the lump in my throat made it hard to answer her. Our kitchen was always messily nice, but somehow it was subtly, wonderfully different today. With us all out of the house this morning, Mum had pottered around, re-acquainting herself with everything. On the table was a bright pink tablecloth, dotted with acid yellow lemons and vivid green limes. I'd forgotten all about that – years ago, when I was pretty little, I used to sit and count the lemons and limes at mealtimes, but always got stuck after I got to twelvety.

And the tablecloth wasn't all... A small, old, cracked vase also sat in the middle of the table, stuffed full of wallflowers and dandelions, and the limp and dried-out herbs in the pots on the windowsill were looking almost perky, after some kind, thoughtful person had bothered to water them. One cupboard door was open, and I could see that Mum had rearranged the tins and packets inside just the way she liked them; not by food group, but by colour.

"You want some?" asked Mum, holding a steaming ladle and pot over the place she'd set for me at the table. She didn't seem to be fazed that I hadn't answered her question.

"Thanks..." I mumbled sheepishly, sitting myself down next to Ivy, who'd already scrambled up on a chair and was wolfing into the great-smelling but sludge-green soup. (What was it made from? *Seaweed*? Some old Cornish recipe for bladderwrack broth or something?)

"It's great, Mum – what is it?" Rowan beamed up at Mum, as the end of one of her plaits dangled precariously close to the green sludge.

"It's courgette and spinach," she explained, dishing out my bowlful. "It's one of Ivy's favourites."

"Yum!" nodded Ivy, happily splashing her blue splodgy Ben drawing with green specks of soup.

"You never made us this before," I wanted to say out loud, but this stupid shyness was strangling the words in my throat again.

"You never made us this before," said Rowan instead (great minds think alike), while her pendulum of a plait swooshed over her soup again.

"Well, I've really got into cooking different things since I left home – since I've been in Cornwall, I mean," Mum corrected herself awkwardly. "My friend Val—"

The phone suddenly tringed loudly into life, interrupting what she was about to tell us.

"I'll get it!" said Rowan, slithering out of her seat and scooting off into the hall.

"My friend Val – she's travelled a lot in Europe and the Far East," Mum continued, pouring herself a bowl of soup and clattering the pot back on to the cooker. "She picked up lots of ideas for cooking and taught them all to me when I was staying with her."

When she turned around, I slurped a mouthful of soup, so that it looked like *that* was my excuse for not responding to her, rather than just this acute, annoying, infuriating shyness getting in my way.

It was totally maddening; here I was, with my mum all to myself for a minute or two (not counting Ivy, Rolf, Winslet and two cats that weren't Colin curled up asleep together in the laundry basket). It was the perfect opportunity to ask her all the questions I had buzzing around in my head, like:

- "How are you and Dad getting along *really*?"
- "Were you upset by Linn last night?"
- "Are you glad to be back, or does it just feel weird?"
- "Do you feel more at home in Cornwall than you do here?"
- "What made you think that we wouldn't want you back?"
- "Have we all changed a lot, since you've been gone?"

Yep, all big, important questions that I desperately wanted the answers to. And instead, what did I finally manage to say?

"So ... um, who's looking after Ben?"

I shouldn't have said this for two reasons:

1) I already knew the answer – Ben was staying with Mum's mate Val while she and Ivy were here; and 2) I started choking when I spoke and shot a fine spray of seaweed – sorry, courgette and spinach – soup out of both nostrils.

Mum had just passed me a piece of kitchen roll and was patting me hard on the back when Rowan walked back in the door, looking like someone had just told her she'd won a thousand pounds and a year's supply of fairy lights or something.

She didn't seem to notice that I'd tried to inhale my soup (and failed miserably), or that the soggy end of one of her plaits was dribbling green gloop down the front of her white school shirt.

"Rowan?" Mum frowned.

"The local paper!" Rowan yelped. "They want to do a story about me! And take my photo! Tomorrow!"

"*Why?*" I managed to ask, with a couple of coughs on either side.

" 'Cause of me being featured in that magazine!" she shrugged, obviously as surprised as I was. "They say, I'm like … like a local celebrity, practically!"

"That's great!" said Mum, clapping her hands together. "But how did they hear about you being in the magazine? I mean, it didn't say in there that you were from round here, did it?"

"I dunno…" Rowan blinked. "But omigod! What am I going to wear!"

And with that she was gone, thundering up the stairs in a panic, about to embark on a *serious* wardrobe rummage.

"I remember once, when she was about six," Mum mused, as she stared after Rowan, "I was taking her out and she changed *fourteen* times before she was happy with her outfit."

"Where were you taking her?" I asked, miraculously managing an entire sentence without embarrassing myself.

"The dentist," Mum turned and grinned at me.

Ah, well, that answered one of my Important Questions (at least in part): in all the years Mum had been away, Rowan *definitely* hadn't changed one little bit…

ICKINESS AND INSPIRATION

Sandie and Billy. The ickiness just *kept* on coming…

"I bought you a present!"

"Aww! You didn't have to buy me a *present*, Billy!"

"But I wanted to!"

"But you don't have to spend all your money on me!"

"But it's only little!"

Sandie stopped protesting, and smiled a mushy smile. "Go on, then! What is it?"

Billy pulled his hand from behind his back and slowly opened his clenched fist.

"Oh, it's *soooo* sweet!" Sandie cooed at the small, slightly melted, white chocolate mouse nestled in Billy's palm.

"I bought it 'cause it reminded me of you!"

What? Sandie reminded Billy of a *mouse*? Or a bit of chocolate? Or something soggy? You know, I don't think I'll *ever* understand this romance thing…

"Oh, Billy, that's *sooooo* cute!" gushed Sandie, her big, blue eyes all sparkle-tastic. "You are *soooo* lovely!"

Urgh – someone pass the sick bucket, *please*…

I know, I know, I *know* I promised to be more understanding and tolerant of my friends' lovey-doveyness, but I made that promise a long, *long* time ago (OK – this *morning*) but now it was the end of the school day and my patience was wearing thin.

So I left Sandie leaning coquettishly on Billy's bike (he'd cycled over madly from the other side of Alexandra Palace just to meet her from school), and shot off home, glad that the presence of Mum and Ivy was a good excuse to leave the lovebirds to it.

And so fifteen minutes speedy walking later, it was goodbye lovebirds and hello lovegod…

Hearing Mum's voice coming from the living room, I'd grabbed the doorframe and swung myself into the room with a big grin on my face, when the shock of seeing Alfie reclining on one of our armchairs nearly made me forget to stop swinging. Luckily, I hauled myself up before I did a full spin and swung my face right into the wall.

"All right, Ally?" Alfie smiled over at me, giving me a hint of a glint of that gold tooth of his. Hey, now *there* was a boy who could buy me a white chocolate mouse *any* time he wanted…

"Yes!" I replied, my voice only a few octaves higher than normal.

I flopped myself as casually as I could on to the sofa, nearly squashing a snoozing cat that wasn't Colin in the process. But with lightning speed and an indignant "pprrrpp!", it leapt to safety (i.e. Alfie's lap) before my bum flattened it.

"You didn't see Linn on your way home, did you, Ally?" asked Mum, as she rearranged the trinkets and candles and bits and bobs on our mantelpiece. "Alfie's arranged to meet her here. They're going round to someone's for tea…"

"Nadia's," Alfie explained, sitting with his legs spread wide (like boys always do, for some strange reason), his scruffy Converse trainers plonked firmly on the floor, where Rolf sat contentedly chewing on a trailing trainer lace.

"No, I haven't seen her," I replied, noticing for the first time that Rowan had beaten me home, and had already changed out of her uniform and was sitting by Tor's old blackboard with Ivy, helping her to create some masterpiece in chalk.

"I was just saying to Alfie that it's funny Linn never mentioned anything about going out for tea tonight!" Mum said directly to me. "She didn't say something to you about it, did she, Ally?"

"*I haven't been here for a long time, and it's only supposed to be a short visit, so I'm pretty disappointed that Linn has chosen to go out tonight...*" was what Mum *really* meant, I was sure.

"Nope, she didn't say anything to me." I shook my head, then noticed something peculiar – Alfie had his gaze fixed directly on Rowan. Poor guy – even though she was looking half-decent right now in a peasanty skirt, vest top and bell-covered belt (part of her outfit for the belly-dancing classes that her and her mate Von went to), I bet a million pounds that Alfie couldn't get that freaky image of her wearing the bikini and apron out of his head. He'd probably have nightmares about it for *weeks*.

Speaking of clothes, what was I doing sitting there in front of Alfie in my bogging school uniform when I had a whole drawerful of excellent T-shirts upstairs? In a nano-second, I'd sprinted off, calling out a muffled "back in a mo" as I ran out of the door and bounded two steps at a time towards my room.

Three minutes and nine changes of T-shirt later (eek! I was turning into Rowan!), I charged panting downstairs and found myself in the middle of a very intriguing conversation.

"It was *you?*" Rowan was saying directly to Alfie, while Ivy hummed a loud tuneless hum and carried on chalking a wavy-edged rainbow on the blackboard.

"You mean, *you* tipped off the local newspaper, Alfie?" Mum blurted out next, standing with her hands on her hips.

What were they all on about? I hovered for a sec, trying to figure out what was going on. (I was worried that asking out loud would have made me sound nosey or thick – or both.)

"Well, yeah…" Alfie shrugged. "My friend Sean's dad works for the paper, and they're always looking for stories. So when I went round to Sean's last night, I, y'know … just sort of *mentioned* to his dad that Rowan had been in that magazine and everything…"

"That's very thoughtful of you!" Mum thanked him, since Rowan was currently staring open-mouthed at him, and didn't seem capable of *moving*, let alone thanking anyone.

Wrong.

In the blink of an eye, she bounced up off the floor and flew across the room, flinging her arms around Alfie and smothering him in a hiccuped "Thank you! Thank you! Thank you!"

Urgh… I admit it; I was jealous. How much

would I have given to have my arms around Alfie like that? All the white chocolate mice in the world…

The only consolation was that Alfie looked vaguely mortified. He was probably worried that he might catch a bad case of ditziness, being in such close proximity to Rowan. Rowan, of course – having only fluff and sequins for brains – didn't even notice his discomfort. She just pulled her arms away, gave him a huge ear-to-ear grin, and flopped back down on the floor beside Ivy.

"I just haven't got a clue what to wear for the photo they're taking tomorrow!" she twittered happily, pulling a pink chalk out from between Winslet's jaws and doodling a heart above Ivy's rainbow.

"Why don't you wear your butterfly jeans, since that's what got you snapped for that magazine in the first place?" Mum suggested.

"'Cause everyone'll have seen that already!" Rowan explained blithely, missing the point that not *everyone* in the cosmiverse reads trendy style and music magazines cover-to-cover. "I really want to come up with something new; customize something else … maybe … maybe like … oh!"

Rowan's hand had frozen in mid-air, still

clutching her piece of chalk, and she was staring at the blackboard.

"I could do *this*! I could do a rainbow!" she announced, sparking back into life and pointing agitatedly at Ivy's colourful stripy doodle. "I could sew a rainbow on to my old denim skirt, using strips of coloured ribbon, or even rows of sequins!"

"But there's not a lot of time to do much sewing, Ro; not if you're getting your photo taken tomorrow after school," Mum pointed out.

"I *could* do it if I used fabric glue, instead of stitching it on. I wonder if I've still got some left...?"

And with that, Rowan was gone in a flurry of inspiration, watched by Mum, Alfie, Ivy and a couple of mildly curious pets.

But *I* wasn't watching her – I was using the opportunity to gawp at Alfie uninterrupted, without anyone noticing.

Except – yikes! – did Mum just catch me there? Oh, the *shame*...!

Chapter 7

HAPPY FAMILIES (ALMOST)

"Right, that's *it*! We've *got* to go and nosey at what's going on!" Salma announced to me over the phone.

"Well, I don't know..." I mumbled uncertainly. "Maybe we'll be in the way."

I wondered why Salma had phoned up tonight for a gossip, since I'd spent both breaks during our first day back at school today doing nothing *but* gossip with her and my other mates. But now I'd sussed it out... She'd obviously mulled over what I'd told her in the afternoon – about Rowan getting interviewed and photographed for the local paper tomorrow after school – and curiosity had got the better of her. She wasn't the only one; I'd already had Kyra on the phone earlier, saying much the same thing – i.e. that we should gatecrash my sister's photoshoot.

"Ally, how can we be in the way?" Salma laughed at me. "You just told me they're going to take her picture in Queen's Woods. How can we get in the way in a huge wood, for goodness' sake?

And anyway, I know it's all above board and everything, but your parents aren't going to let Rowan go on her own are they? So we'll be like a ... what do you call it ... chaperone!"

"Yeah, I guess," I shrugged, knowing that I had practically *no* chance of dissuading either Kyra or Salma. And hopefully, Rowan wouldn't mind having the three of us there, just to show her some support, or be her chaperone or whatever.

"Tell you what ... I've had a great idea!" said Salma, in a tone of voice that spelt trouble. "I'll take the monsters with me, and *you* take Ivy – I'm dying to meet her, and she'll get on brilliantly with my lot, since they're the same age!"

The "monsters" were Salma's tiny twin sisters, Rosa and Julia, plus her niece Laurel, who was so identical to Julia and Rosa that they could have been triplets. The three of them were very cute; at least they were when they stayed still and silent, which they never did. I had no idea what Ivy would make of these mini-tornadoes.

"What was that sigh for, Ally? Don't you think that's a good idea?"

I didn't realize I'd sighed out loud – I thought I'd only done it in my head. Did that mean that when I sighed with unrequited love whenever Alfie was around, everyone heard that too? Gulp...

"It's just... It's just that it's going to get complicated," I started to explain. "If I take Ivy, then Tor'll want to come, and if Tor comes, he'll want to take the dogs, seeing as we're going to the woods."

"So?" said Salma, not seeing any problem with that.

The problem was that – no matter how big Queen's Woods were – three gawping teenagers, four small yelping children, one bouncing seven-year-old boy and two hyperactive dogs might *just* distract Rowan a little bit. I might as well put posters up everywhere and invite the whole of Crouch End along.

"Look, I'll have to check it's OK with Ro first," I told Salma, as I peered up the stairs in the direction of Rowan's room and the sound of the weird Arabic belly-dancing music she was listening to in there, while she was frantically sticking ribbon rainbows on her skirt.

"She won't mind!" Salma said assuredly. "Anyway, got to go – Rosa's just pulled the head off Julia's doll. No! No, Rosa! *Don't* try and stuff it in the toaster!"

The phone clattered off at her end, as Salma went to rescue Julia's doll and the whole family from a month's worth of toast that smelt of melted plastic. For a second, I thought about going and chatting with Rowan about this photoshoot business, but just as I was about to head up the cat-covered stairs, I heard Dad's voice launch into a story I hadn't heard him read for years. It was from a picture book that had started out as Linn's, and been read to every Love child in turn over the years. Looked like it was Ivy's turn now...

"*'It's such a lovely day – what shall we do, Sammy?' asked Peter the Penguin.*"

As I pushed open the living-room door, I saw a pretty nice scene. Mum was curled up on one of the armchairs, hugging one of her own wonky handmade mugs and a cat that wasn't Colin, and smiling over at Dad, Ivy, Tor and Rolf, who were all piled up on the sofa together in a tangle of arms, legs, Spiderman jim-jams (Tor's), pink bunny-suits (Ivy's) and fur (Rolf's).

"*'I know what we can do!' said Sammy. 'We can have a picnic right here!'*" Dad read aloud from the battered book which he was resting on Rolf's hairy tummy.

"Where did you find that?" I interrupted, leaning on the back of the sofa and ruffling Tor's head.

"I spotted it on the bottom shelf of Tor's bookshelf last night. Ow!" Dad turned his head to explain, then rubbed his neck in pain.

"What's wrong?" asked Mum in alarm.

"Oh, just a crick in my neck from that blow-up bed," said Dad, rolling his head around in a circle to loosen his neck. "Guess I maybe need to blow it up more, eh, Tor!"

Dad had been sleeping in Tor's bedroom for the last three nights, while Mum and Ivy curled up in the big double bed in Dad's room. Mum and Dad's room, I mean. But I actually don't think he'd been doing much sleeping, by the looks of the dark circles under his eyes. A deflating bed and a room full of small, nocturnal animals that get frisky by night meant not too many sweet dreams for Dad.

"More story!" Ivy piped up suddenly.

"Ivy!" Mum said in a cautionary tone.

"More story, *pease*!" Ivy corrected herself (nearly).

"Tell you what! Why don't we finish this upstairs?" Dad suggested, gently trying to disentangle himself from the arms, legs and fur so that he could stand up. Like the Pied Piper, he led the way out of the living-room door, followed in descending order of height by Tor, Rolf, Ivy, Winslet and a curious cat that wasn't Colin.

"I'd forgotten all about that book!" I smiled, grabbing my chance to get the sofa to myself (a very rare occurrence in our crowded house).

"I remember when Rowan was little, she always used to cry at the bit when Willie the Whale got sad that he couldn't come out of the water and get up on the beach to join in the picnic!" Mum reminisced, with her hand still hovering in the air after waving Tor and Ivy off to bed.

"Did she?" I grinned.

Not that it was any big surprise to hear that Rowan had cried at something. If Linn was the Grouch Queen of Crouch End, then Rowan was the Princess of Blubbing. She could turn on the tears in a nano-second, crying if she was extra-upset *or* extra-happy. It's like when she's watching TV, she can cry at sad endings, happy endings, at depressing stories on the news, or the sight of cute puppies on Rolf's *Animal Hospital*. But then she has this amazing ability to stop crying just as quickly. It's like last week – she was in floods at the end of this movie when the hero died, and then was smiling and asking who wanted any Raspberry Ripple ice-cream as soon as the credits began to roll.

"Speaking of Rowan..." Mum said, all of a sudden, "...what about Alfie?"

The blood in my veins turned ice-lolly cold. I was sure Mum had caught me drooling over Alfie earlier – was that what she was getting at? Y'know, for a moment there, I'd stopped being shy with

Mum (hurrah!), but now that she'd brought up the matter of you-know-who and stupid-lovelorn-me, I instantly felt all that shyness come swooping *straight* back.

"Alfie? Um... It was... It was really nice of him to get Rowan in the paper!" I waffled, trying to pretend I didn't know what she was getting at, while feeling my face flush telltale crimson.

"So, are you thinking what *I'm* thinking, Ally?" she beamed, her green eyes twinkling mischievously.

Oh, how embarrassing. Mum had only been back home about five minutes and she'd already sussed my crush on Alfie. *Please* don't let her have mentioned it to Linn – my life wouldn't be worth living... (Still, the fact that Linn and Mum hadn't exactly been bonding in a warm mother–daughter way probably meant that my secret was safe for the time being.)

"Er ... what are *you* thinking?" I asked Mum, playing for time while I felt myself get so hot with shame that I was practically on the verge of self-combusting.

"Alfie..." she grinned. "He's got a real crush on Rowan, hasn't he?"

Well, knock me down with a feather. Or make that a sackful. *Alfie* ... fancying *Rowan*?! Was Mum *kidding*?

"Mum, he thinks she's a ... a *fruitcake*!" I found myself blurting out.

"Well, maybe he likes fruitcake!" she smiled knowingly.

Good grief – Mum's romance radar was *so* not working. I mean, how much more wrong could she be?

Me and Linn and Rowan – we all love each other, even if Linn doesn't love me and Ro very much when we nick her special treats out of the fridge (we pretend we can't read the "Property of Linn Love" stickers she puts on them). And then again, Linn is kind of hard to love when she's in one of her (near-constant) grouches. But love stuff aside, deep down, sisters are meant to have special bonds, aren't they? Like spooky psychic links with each other?

Well, normally, I wouldn't say that me, Rowan and Linn shared particularly special bonds or whatever, but at 10.30 p.m. that Tuesday night, our *bladders* seemed to be psychically linked, that's for sure. Which is why, when I padded down the darkened stairs to the bathroom, I found my two older sisters had already beaten me to it. From the way they were standing, it looked like Rowan was coming out and Linn was about to go in, only the changeover had been postponed while they had a heated, whispered conversation.

And uh-oh ... Rowan was snivelling.

"What's wrong?" I joined in the whispering, not wanting to wake up a snoozling Tor or Ivy. (There was a chink of light showing at the living room downstairs, so Mum and Dad were probably still up.)

"It's *her*!" Linn hissed, pointing a finger at Rowan. "She's living in La-La Land!"

Well, we all knew Rowan was a bit of a space cadet, but so what? I frowned at Linn, wondering what she was getting at.

"I just told Linn that before I came to bed, I saw Mum and Dad in the garden, talking in the dark!" Rowan sniffled.

"Um ... *so*?" I shrugged.

"So she thinks that's terribly romantic," Linn replied, rolling her eyes. "She thinks that's a sure sign that they're definitely back together. And now she's got all upset 'cause I told her not to bet on it!"

"*You* think they're going to get back together, don't you, Al?" Rowan asked me, her eyes brimming with yet more tears, and a trickle of snot quivering on her top lip.

"Oh, grow up, Ro!" Linn snarled softly, before I got a chance to answer.

"Why are you being so horrible?" I suddenly found myself snapping at Linn. (Not something I normally do – it's not perfect, but I quite like my head and don't fancy it being torn from my body by an irate older sister.)

"I'm not being *horrible*, I'm being *realistic*," Linn hissed in her defence. "What's the point in getting used to having Mum around when she'll probably be going back to Cornwall any day now?"

"But why should she?" I quizzed Linn.

"And why *shouldn't* she?" Linn countered. "When I spoke to Dad earlier, he admitted he didn't know what was going to happen, which doesn't exactly sound too promising!"

"When did he say that?" I whispered, feeling an icy chill sweep up my back that had nothing to do with the zillions of draughts that regularly whirl round our wonky old house.

"When I was round at the shop today, after school."

So *that's* why she'd been late meeting Alfie.

"Why did you go round to the shop?" I asked next, knowing it wasn't really Linn's style to hang out with Dad and his beloved assortment of half-mended bikes. (Nothing against Dad – it was just that the shop was *way* too oily and messy for Linn's liking.)

"Dad asked me to," said Linn, dropping her gaze to the floor. "He wanted to talk to me about ... Mum and how I was getting on with her and stuff."

A-ha – it didn't take a genius (and trust me, I'm *not* one), to work out what that translated as: Dad had picked up on every little barbed comment of Linn's yesterday, and had wanted to have a quiet word with her about it. Yikes – Linn wouldn't have liked being hauled up by Dad one little bit. No wonder she was grouchy times ten tonight.

"Anyway, we talked about ... stuff," Linn said vaguely, brushing a stray wisp of blondey hair behind her ear, "and that's when he said that he didn't know how things would work out. Which is what I was trying to tell Rowan just now, so she wouldn't get her hopes up. But then she goes and starts blubbing, *as* usual!"

"Everything all right up there?" Mum's voice suddenly drifted up the stairs, as a blast of light shone out of the newly opened living-room door.

"Yes!" we all replied in unison (spooky sisterly bonds in action again).

And in two seconds flat Rowan had disappeared into her room, Linn had vanished into the bathroom, and I found myself sitting on a darkened stair, waiting my turn for the loo, wondering and worrying that Mum might have heard more of our conversation than was good for her...

Chapter 8

SNAPPY SURPRISES

"Why have you got so much make-up on?" Kyra asked Salma bluntly.

"It's hardly anything!" Salma protested, tossing back her gorgeous, shiny, long dark hair. "It's only lip-gloss!"

"*And* the rest!" Kyra sniggered. "You've put it on with a shovel! *And* you're wearing your best clothes!"

"Am not!" Salma frowned, glancing down at her new wine-coloured cord jeans and her favourite, deep-pink satin T-shirt. "It's just that everything else was in the wash!"

"*Liar!* You're all glammed up 'cause you're hoping that photographer woman spots you and asks to take your picture too!" Kyra niggled at her.

"Am not!" Salma snapped back, not sounding too convincing.

"Are too! Look, that woman only works for the local newspaper – she's not a talent scout for Premier Model Agency or anything! Face it, Sal – as soon as she's finished here, she'll probably be zooming off to take a picture of a broken sewage pipe in the high street!"

You know, Kyra was probably right: Salma *was* awfully glammed up for hanging out in the woods. Still, with Kyra, you always have the funny feeling that she gets a real kick out of seeing the worst in people.

It's the total opposite with my mum; she's the sort of person that always tries to find nice things to say about practically everyone. And Mum could be friends with practically anyone too, even if they had practically nothing in common. It was like that with Billy's mother – my mum and Mrs Stevenson got to be matey 'cause me and *him* were, even though *my* mum was this laid-back hippy and *his* was this uptight neat-freak.

Anyhow – speaking of neat-freaks – this afternoon Mrs Stevenson had appeared at our doorstep in her neat business suit, neat hairsprayed hairdo and a waft of posh perfume. Naturally, Billy had told her that Mum had turned up out of the blue, and she'd been desperate to come round for a coffee and a very large catch-up with her. So it was perfect, really, that I'd gathered up Tor and Ivy and the dogs and taken them out to Rowan's photoshoot in Queen's Woods, leaving them in peace to chat.

And luckily, Rowan was so thrilled about posing

in her newly customized rainbow skirt on a gnarled tree stump that she didn't seem in the least bit bothered that Salma's little monsters and Ivy were now shrieking their way around some nearby trees, chased by Tor and our happily barking dogs. Or that me, Kyra and Salma were hovering around, checking out the action (when Kyra and Salma weren't too busy bickering, of course). And that's not even counting Billy and Sandie, who'd turned up too, saying they were "just passing". Ha! Who were they kidding? "Just noseying", more like...

And then there was one more person here too ... someone I *definitely* hadn't expected to see.

"Go and ask him!" Kyra goaded me, digging me in the ribs with her annoyingly sharp elbow, now that she'd got fed up with teasing Salma. "Ask him what he's doing here!"

"No!" I hissed back, flashing my eyes at her, hoping she picked up the message I was trying to telepathically *sear* into her mind. The message read: "*Please* stop trying to get me to go over and talk to Alfie! You *know* I'll only turn bright red, and then *everyone* will guess that I fancy him!"

Yep, there was the object of my affection, fumbling around in a big canvas bag after giving me a wave and a smile hello. (Be still, my beating heart!) I had no idea what Alfie was doing here; the only thing I was sure of was that only Sandie and Kyra knew that I had a crush on him as big as Alaska, and that's *exactly* how I wanted it to stay, thank you very much.

"Well, *I'll* go and ask him, then!" Billy said blithely, letting go of Sandie's hand and stomping across the crunchy bed of leaves and twigs towards Alfie.

"Oh, come on! We'll *all* go!" Kyra announced, clasping me by the arm and forcing me towards Alfie, as Sandie and Salma trotted behind us.

"Alfie's taking photos of Rowan too!" Billy announced to us, pointing to the camera Alfie had just pulled from his canvas bag.

"For part of my A-level Art coursework," Alfie chipped in, pushing up the long sleeves of his top and revealing his skinny but muscly arms.

I glanced over at Rowan, to see if she had any clue that Alfie was going to turn up here, but she was too busy following the real photographer's instructions and holding on to a low-hanging tree branch picturesquely.

"Hey – look who's just arrived!" said Sandie, grabbing my attention with a nudge and nodding in the direction of the path that leads into the woods from the road. Three girls were strolling towards us; Nadia, Mary and...

"Hi, Linn!" Alfie, called out, spotting my eldest sister and her mates at the same as the rest of us, and walking towards her.

Linn may have lost her temper a bit with Rowan last night, but curiosity must have got the better of her. Still, like me, she hadn't exactly expected to see Alfie at Rowan's shoot.

"What are *you* doing here?" she frowned directly at him.

"Ouch! What's *her* problem?" Kyra mumbled in my ear, in one of her famous not-very-quiet whispers. "Is she *jealous* or something?"

"Jealous? How do you mean?" I whispered back. As far as I could see, Linn was just grouchy, and there was nothing new in *that*.

"I know they're just supposed to be mates..." Kyra said with a shrug, studying my big sister's body language, "...but Linn looks *well* hacked off. D'you think she secretly fancies Alfie?"

Much as I hated to admit it, maybe Kyra was a better judge of lovey-doveyness than Mum; after all, last night Mum was *way* off the case when she suggested that Alfie had the hots for Ro. But weirdly enough, maybe Kyra had a point about Linn's feelings for Alfie.

From the look on her face right now, Linn was one *very* unhappy bunny...

ONE LONG LIST AND A LOVE BITE

I don't know quite how Linn managed to get home before us (flew home on her broomstick, maybe?), but when me and Tor and Ivy and the dogs came tumbling into the kitchen, there she was, slamming her way around the cupboards.

"God! You can't find *anything* in this place anymore!" she growled, staring at a colour-coded pile of tins and packets that ranged from red (i.e. chopped tomatoes) to orange (i.e. beans) to yellow (i.e. sweetcorn).

"What are you looking for, Linn, and maybe I can help?" said a startled-looking Mum, glancing up from the pot she was stirring.

"Doesn't matter..." Linn replied glumly, before stomping out of the room.

Luckily, Ivy and Tor hadn't witnessed any of Linn's growling; no sooner had they arrived in the kitchen than they'd zoomed out to play in the garden with Rolf and Winslet. But *I'd* seen it, and so had Mum...

"Oh, Ally...!" she sighed sadly, folding her arms across her chest and dropping her gaze to the floor.

I had a horrible feeling that she might be going to cry. All I wanted to do was rush over and give her a cuddle, but a familiar wave of shyness suddenly washed over me, rooting me to the spot as sure as if someone had pinned my trainers to the floor with a staple gun.

"This is all much harder than I thought!"

"Um... Linn you mean?" I answered Mum, panicking at the wobble I'd heard in her voice. "It's not you! She's in a mood with Alfie!"

I thought Mum might ask more about that, but instead, she turned towards me, gave me a watery smile and said: "It's not just Linn. Do you know Tor's friend Freddie?"

I nodded. Freddie was one of Tor's best mates.

"Well, when I went to pick up Tor from school today, you know what Freddie told me?"

I shook my head, watching as Mum pushed her long wild mane of hair back off her troubled face.

"Tor forgot his drawing, and when he ran back into the classroom for it, Freddie told me that Tor thought I was 'cool', but not as 'cool' as Daisy from his summer school."

Urgh... I guess that's not what Mum wanted to hear – that her little boy preferred another woman to her. Specially another woman who Dad had been "friends" with.

"Oh, don't mind me, Ally!" she tried to laugh. "I'm just being silly!"

I wanted to tell her that she wasn't being silly, and that maybe everything *was* kind of weird, but that it was bound to be at first. But I couldn't tell her that because the words might have been clear and ordered in my head but I couldn't seem to get them out of my mouth. And anyway, a clatter of four feet and eight paws interrupted us.

"I taught Ivy stuff!" Tor announced.

Despite how wibbly-wobbly she'd sounded a second ago, Mum swapped a hint of a smile with me, before saying, "Really, what's that, then?"

"All the names of all the pets!" said Tor proudly.

"What; you've taught Ivy them *all*?" I asked incredulously. I mean, we have a *serious* amount of pets.

Tor nodded.

"What – you taught her them all just *now*?" Mum quizzed him.

"No ... we've been practising," shrugged Tor casually, while Ivy stood by his side, blinking her huge brown eyes at her big bruv.

Wow ... was this possible? Was this small person – who looked like a mini-Tor, only with a bob hairdo and dressed all in pink – about to startle us with her uncanny memory skills? Good grief; did we have a child *genius* in the family?

Well, not *quite*.

"Say it after me, Ivy," Tor instructed her. "Rolf..."

"Olf!" Ivy squealed eagerly, as Rolf snuffled half a bark beside her.

"Winslet..."

"Winnit!" she repeated, getting a gruff snort from Winslet too.

"Colin..."

"Conin!"

"And how many legs does Colin have?" Tor sidetracked for a second, in his best schoolteacher voice.

Ivy frowned momentarily, then piped up, "Two!"

"No, *three*," Tor corrected Ivy.

I glanced at Mum and saw that she was struggling, same as me, not to laugh.

"Then there's Derek..."

"Drek!"

"Eddie..."

"Teddy!"

"No – *Eddie*, not *Teddy*..."

"I like Teddy!"

"OK, whatever. Then there's Fluffy..."

"Fuffy!"

You know, cute as it was, and amazing as it was to hear so much of Ivy's voice in one go, there are *so* many animals squeaking and barking and snurfling around in our house that it took Tor and Ivy about six *months* to get through the whole squeaking, barking, snurfling lot of them. By the time they'd got to the stick insects, I'd just about lost the will to *live*.

"Brian..."

"Brian!"

Brian? I mused to myself, my fixed grin starting to ache. *Since when did a stick insect suit the name "Brian"?*

"Domino..."

"Donimo!"

"Zebedee..."

"Zedabee!"

Winslet and Rolf were lying comatose on the kitchen floor now, I noticed, lulled into a state of unconsciousness with the dullness of the never-ending list of names.

"Brooklyn..."

"Booklyn!"

"Romeo..."

"Actually, I better go upstairs and do my homework," I muttered, backing my way out of the kitchen door, while giving Mum an apologetic smile.

You know, I never thought I'd be so glad to see a maths equation...

Course, I wasn't so fond of maths equations half an hour later, when they were totally doing my head in.

The only thing that was going to get me through my homework (and tide me over till tea was ready) was to get myself a small chocolate something out of the biscuit tin.

I'd just come out of my room and was about to head down the stairs in the direction of the kitchen, when I peeked in through Linn's slightly open bedroom door, and saw her kneeling on her window seat, gazing down into the garden below.

"What are you looking at?" I asked, hovering in the doorway, since Linn didn't really like anyone that hadn't been steam-cleaned and decontaminated invading the sanctity of her perfect room.

"Mum and Dad... They're over by the swing ... talking."

She didn't tell me to go away and close the door while I was at it, so I took that as the closest I'd get to an invitation to come in.

"What do you think they're talking about?" I

asked, treading softly over her immaculate cream carpet, and hoping I didn't have any traces of Queen's Woods mud still stuck in the ridges of my trainers.

"Guess they're talking about all of us, I s'pose," she replied, her eyes still fixed on a point out in the garden.

Tentatively, I knelt beside her on the window seat and peeked down. Mum and Dad were leaning on either side of the swing, talking, listening, and not doing much smiling, by the looks of it. Bummer.

"Er..." I began to say, taking my life in my hands, "...don't you think—"

The rest of that sentence was "...you're not really helping things by being snippy with Mum?" but a thundering of feet hammering up the attic stairs put paid to that. Probably just as well, for my physical well-being.

"Oh, you're in here, Al!" Rowan panted at the door. "What are you two doing?"

"Watching Mum and Dad," I told her.

"Yeah?" she said breathlessly, walking into the hallowed ground of Linn's room and hoisting up her denim skirt to kneel beside us on the now-cramped window seat. "What are they doing?"

"Nothing. Just talking," Linn mumbled, still staring outside.

"Are you just back from Queen's Woods?"

As I asked that, I reached over and pulled a rogue twig out of Rowan's crimped hair.

"Uh-huh. I had the best time!"

I felt Linn twitch imperceptibly beside me, before she hit Rowan with a question of her own.

"Did … did Alfie take a lot of photos, then?"

My ears strained to hear if there was a definite edge of jealousy in Linn's voice, but I couldn't be sure.

"I suppose – I don't know really, I wasn't counting," Rowan shrugged beside me. "Don't you think Mum and Dad look a bit serious?"

"Not especially," Linn replied. "So, was the newspaper photographer there all this time too?"

"No … she went away ages ago."

There – *there* was Linn doing that twitching thing again. She *really* didn't seem to like the fact that Rowan and Alfie had been on their own together. That had to be a sign of jealousy, right?

"Are you sure they're OK down there?" Rowan frowned, steaming up a pane of glass with her concerned words. "They look pretty serious to me!"

"What we need is a lip-reader!" I joked lamely, darting my eyes towards Rowan to see if I'd managed to squeeze a smile out of her.

And then I saw something. On Ro's neck. A pinky-red bruise, plain as day.

It couldn't be... I mean, it wasn't... I mean, that was a *love bite*, wasn't it...?

Chapter 10

FRETTING, WORRYING AND BISCUITS

A shaft of moonlight spilled into my attic bedroom, which was very poetic and beautiful and everything, only I wasn't in the mood to take much notice of its poetic beauty 'cause I was too busy lying awake wondering if that really *was* a love bite I'd seen on Rowan's neck.

It could have been a shadow, right? Or some trick of the light? You know – sunshine refracting off a silvery plane wing passing overhead, causing a beam of light to shoot through the glass pane in Linn's window and casting this rainbow of colour, so that Rowan ended up with what *looked* like patch of pink on her neck. Or something.

OK, so I didn't know what *exactly* I'd seen earlier this evening. And hey, you never know – it could've just been a smudge of dirt. 'Cause not so long ago, I remembered Linn accusing *me* of having a love bite, and all it was was a blob of mud after me and Billy (the big berk) had a fun fight in the park at Alexandra Palace. So maybe it was just mud *I* spotted tonight. It really *couldn't* have been a love bite, could it? The only way that was possible was for Ro to have been given a love bite by: a) the photographer from the local newspaper, who was about 112 and a *woman*, for goodness' sake; or b) Alfie. And considering that Alfie and Rowan had known each other for years and had never taken the slightest bit of notice of each other in all that time, it wasn't exactly likely that they'd fall instantly in lust with each other, just like *that*, was it?

So there you go. It *couldn't* have been a love bite. Could it…?

This was getting me nowhere, and it certainly wasn't getting me to sleep. There was only one thing for it; a midnight snack. Milk and biccies, here I come…

But two minutes later, my overpowering need for milk and biccies had evaporated. After padding my way down two flights of stairs, I was now hovering outside the living-room door, listening into something I most definitely wasn't meant to hear.

"But they're all so grown-up! They don't need me!"

"That's not true, Melanie!"

"Yes, it is, Martin! They've got you, they've got their gran, they've got each other… They've learnt to manage without me – which is all my own fault, and I know it!"

"But—"

"But nothing! You just need to look at Linn and you see how hard it is for her to accept me even *being* here!"

"Look, both of us knew this wasn't going to be easy…"

Dad might have been in the middle of a pretty fraught conversation with Mum, but a creak or two of the floorboards inside the room alerted me to the fact that he was ominously close to the door, and the last thing I wanted was to be caught listening in to what they were saying, even if it did involve us.

I toyed with zipping back up the stairs, but if Dad flung open the door right that second, I'd be caught halfway up them. So, with my heart hammering, I turned and tiptoed at top speed towards the kitchen, nearly tripping over a couple of hairy dogs in the process.

On automatic pilot, I pulled open the fridge and grabbed a plastic container. Nibbling on a biscuit I wasn't even tasting, I poured a big glass of milk, all the while asking myself, "Will it be OK with Mum and Dad?" over and over again in my scrambled brain.

"Oh, hello, Ally Pally! I didn't know you were down here!"

Dad's voice made me jump, as if I was guilty of sneaking in the back door with a swag bag.

"Bit 'ungry," I mumbled through a mouthful of chocolate Digestive.

"Bit thirsty!" he smiled back at me, flicking on the kettle and pulling two cups out of the cupboard. "You want one?"

"Nah," I shook my head, pointing to my glass of milk.

I noticed that Dad's short, curly hair was standing up on top, like a mad little quiff. That meant he'd been running his fingers through it, and he only did that when he was worried or daydreaming, and somehow – from the snatch of conversation *I'd* caught – I didn't think he'd been doing much daydreaming this evening. And another thing I noticed ... Dad's always pretty skinny, but under his faded grey T-shirt and jeans, he looked ... almost *bonier* than usual.

"Biscuit?" I said, spraying crumbs as I spoke. Maybe I couldn't make the situation any easier, but I could always try and feed him up a bit.

"No, thanks, hon, I'm not hungry."

Neither of us spoke for a moment, with only the whoosh of the kettle and crunching of my biscuit breaking the silence. Until...

"Me and your mum, we're just having a chat,

you know," Dad said casually (or at least what he *thought* was casually), as he dropped teabags into the mugs. "Um, you didn't hear any of it, did you?"

I opened my eyes wide, feigning innocence, and shook my head from side to side. If I'd tried to talk, I might have choked on my biscuit, which would have served me right for lying.

"Everything will be all right, you know, Ally Pally," Dad said softly, shooting me a meaningful look, except I was too worried to understand the meaning of it. "However this works out, you'll never lose touch with your mum again."

"Oh. OK."

To be honest, I *still* didn't understand quite what that meant, but I tried to allow myself to be slightly reassured.

"Anyway, I've got a favour to ask... I was thinking that maybe it would be good for me and Mum to go out on our own for a nice dinner somewhere tomorrow night. Would it be all right if you and your sisters kept an eye on Tor and Ivy?"

"Sure," I smiled shyly, a tiny glimmer of hope twinkling in my head. A romantic dinner out might be *exactly* what Mum and Dad needed. And Dad *actually* eating something would be pretty good too...

I gave him a peck on the cheek and scooted out of the kitchen with my glass of milk and a couple more biscuits. As I bounded silently up the stairs, I gave a quick backward glance at the closed living-room door, feeling a bit more optimistic than I had when I was standing outside it a few minutes ago.

And then on the first landing, a certain snuffling made me stop in my tracks. Or maybe it was more that it was an *uncertain* snuffling: it didn't sound like one of the cats or dogs, and it wasn't one of the hamsters or mice or gerbils or whatever 'cause the uncertain snuffling was coming from the direction of Dad's room, not Tor's.

"Ivy?" I called out softly, pushing the door open.

It didn't look as if Ivy liked the dark too much – Mum had left a small lamp switched on over on the dressing table, which cast a warm orange glow over the whole (orange-painted) room. And there, under the orange duvet, was a small bump of a small body, with only a brown fringe, watery eyes and a runny nose peeking out on the pillow.

"Hey, what's up?" I asked, dumping my milk and cookies on the bedside table and sitting down beside her. "Are you feeling sad?"

Ivy wriggled herself into a more upright position and nodded.

I yanked a tissue out of the box by the bed and helped her dab at her nose, which she parped noisily.

"So what's making you sad?" I asked her. She was too young to pick up on all the uncertainty with Mum and Dad, wasn't she? Maybe she was just feeling homesick...

"I wan' Ben!" she muttered in a teeny-tiny voice, proving me right. (OK, so it was more *dog*-sickness than *home*sickness.)

At first, I wasn't sure what to say. "Don't worry, you'll see him soon"? Well, I actually didn't *want* to say that, because I didn't *want* Ivy or Mum to go back to Cornwall any time soon... If I had my way, they'd stay put here with us for ever and ever. If not longer.

And then I remembered something.

"Hey, I know a song called 'Ben'!" I told her, an ancient tune by Michael Jackson popping to the forefront of my mind.

"Me too!" Ivy piped up, a smile thankfully pinging on to her face.

Wow ... that song was on some old vinyl album of Mum's that she sometimes played when we were young. Did she have another copy of it now – maybe on CD – that Ivy had heard?

"Shall we sing it? To remind you of Ben?" I suggested.

Ivy nodded at top speed, delighted at this idea.

"OK!" I grinned back, thrilled to have been able to cheer her up. "How does it go again? '*Ben…*'"

Just as I sang the first word (with Ivy trilling along too), I realized two things:

1) The song "Ben", is actually about a pet rat, not a pet dog; and…

2) I couldn't remember any of the words to it apart from … er … "*Ben*".

Luckily, Ivy didn't care about either point, and seemed quite happy to sing along with the fantastic words I'd substituted.

And so, for the next ten minutes we happily sang "*Ben, la, la, laaa, Ben, Ben, Ben, Ben!*" over and over again, till *I* was the only one singing and Ivy was fast asleep…

Chapter 11

CODED CONVERSATIONS

"Mmmmfffff-*ppppprrrriiinnnnggg*!!"

The problem with having your alarm clock wrapped up in a dressing gown in the bottom of your wardrobe is that it's a real pain in the neck trying to turn the thing off.

This Thursday morning was no exception – in fact it was harder than usual 'cause I was pooped after my disturbed night of fretting, worrying, biscuit-eating and song-singing. (I vaguely remember being woken by Mum in that warm orange room and gently led upstairs to my own bed at some point in the night.)

And so today, as soon as that distant "Mmmmfffff-*ppppprrrriiinnnnggg*!!" went off, I leapt up out of bed in a grump, landing flat on my face with my duvet wrapped around my legs, and came face-to-face with a hairball some cat had coughed up on the carpet. (Blee...) And the first three-quarters of an hour of my day weren't much better. Somehow I managed to: a) be last in the shower (mmm, icy water, how refreshing!); b) dip the end of my tie in my orange juice (had to suck it out); c) lose one of my school shoes (anyone know what could have happened to that? Eh, Winslet?).

"Tor, have you seen my other shoe?" I asked, hovering lopsided in the living room.

"Nope," said Tor, sounding strangely nasal, but that's maybe because he was upside down. I don't know *why* Tor (dressed in grey trousers and school sweatshirt) and Ivy (still in her pink bunny-suit) were sitting topsy-turvy on the sofa, watching an old episode of the *Teletubbies* with their legs pointing roof-wards and their heads dangling over the edge of the cushions. But I guess it's a good way of making repeats on TV seem more interesting.

Leaving them to it (whatever "it" was), I continued my search elsewhere.

"Rolf – have you seen my other shoe, or Winslet, for that matter?" I asked the hairy mutt that was comfortably stretched out, blocking the whole of the hallway widthways, as I limped my way towards the kitchen.

In reply, Rolf carried on snoring, his tummy full of dog food and leftover toast, and his doggy brain switched to the "off" position. Maybe the other – less furry – members of my family would be of more help, and at least three of them were now to be found in the kitchen. Dad was busy drying off the pan the beans had been in, Linn was smoothing down her already immaculately smooth hair in the mirror by the message board, and Rowan was wiping breakfast crumbs off the kitchen table, gliding the damp cloth around a happily purring Colin.

"Hey, any of you happen to have seen my other shoe? Looks kind of like this one?" I said, pointing down to my left leg.

"Ah, Ally!" Dad muttered at the sight of me, ignoring my so-called joke and hurrying over to close the door behind me. "Now that I've got all you girls together…"

Hmm – didn't like the sound of *that* too much. Neither did Linn or Rowan; Linn stopped fiddling with her hair and was oblivious to a wispy curl gently unwhirling itself from her neat, stubby ponytail, and Rowan accidentally wiped the damp cloth towards herself, sending a sprinkle of soggy crumbs on to her skirt.

"…I just wanted to say something."

About Mum, obviously. Otherwise, Dad wouldn't have closed the kitchen door while Mum was upstairs pottering about, and he wouldn't be speaking in this funny hushed tone.

"The thing is … the thing *is*, Mum's feeling a bit out of sorts at the moment. Being back here and everything," Dad began, the dark shadows still apparent under his brown eyes.

Urgh. Was this the start of him explaining that she'd decided to go away again? Oh, please, oh, please, oh, *please* don't let that be the case…

"Doesn't she like being with us?" asked Ro, blinking her newly mascara'd eyes rapidly. (Uh-oh – blubbing alert…)

"Oh, *yes*! Yes, of *course* she does!" Dad whispered urgently, spotting that he may not have phrased his last comment too well. "She's absolutely *loving* seeing all of you again! It's just that it's hard for her … fitting in, I mean, after being gone so long."

Rowan was still blinking – tears only nano-seconds away – while Linn and me stayed mute.

"What I'm saying is," Dad blustered on, in the vacuum of our silence, "well, what I'm *trying* to say is, I know it's a bit weird for all of us, and everyone is doing a *great* job, but could you girls go out of your way to make Mum feel *extra*-welcome over the next few days?"

At first, I felt swamped with guilt; if only I could relax when I was with Mum, and start acting *more* like a daughter and *less* like a shy little schoolgirl stuck in front of the headmistress, then she'd be *sure* to stay. And *then* I thought, OK, so *I* hadn't been perfect, but why was Dad having a go at Rowan? What could Ro possibly do to make Mum feel more welcome, short of chucking rose petals in front of her when she walked? Out of all of us Love children, she'd been the most overpoweringly happy to have Mum home, constantly hanging out with her, chattering away so madly that you'd think she was desperately trying to pack in four *years'* worth of chattering in one go.

But – *wham!* – suddenly I realized Dad was speaking in code; he might have been addressing this request to all of us, but it was mostly meant for *Linn*, I was sure. 'Cause even after their little talk together round Dad's shop on Tuesday – whatever that had involved – Linn still seemed to be having a problem being civil to Mum; like that business of clattering around in the kitchen cupboards last night, moaning about Mum rearranging everything. I'd fibbed to Mum when I'd tried to tell her it was more about Linn being mad with Alfie. OK, so that hadn't exactly helped Linn's mood, but basically, it was still just another example of Linn being grouchy with Mum. (And why *that* was, I still had no idea, and was *way* too cowardly to ask her…)

"Anyway, Mum and I are going out for a meal

tonight, and Ally's already offered to babysit," Dad continued. "But Mum's going to the hairdresser later this afternoon, so can one of you pick Tor up from school?"

"I can't!" Rowan blurted out, the threat of tears miraculously vanishing. "I've got ... um ... something to do..."

From a blurt to a mumble. What was that all about? And why did she seem to be blushing as pink as a stick of rhubarb all of a sudden?

Ro's instant rosy cheeks weren't lost on Linn either. She gave our in-between sister a narrow-eyed stare while telling Dad that of course she'd pick up Tor, no problem.

But whatever secrets and undercurrents and coded conversations were bubbling in our kitchen this morning, something far more down-to-earth and straightforward suddenly grabbed my attention.

"Winslet!" I yelled out the window, spotting a blur of digging legs, a flurry of earth, and something chunky and black being buried at the back of the garden. (Ah, well – first time this term...!)

Chapter 12

KISSING WITH TONGUES (BLEE!)

"Isn't Sandie supposed to be shy?" asked Kyra, folding her arms across her chest, and studying what was going on at the bus stop across the road from the school gate.

Sandie was waiting for the bus to take her up to the Broadway and her dentist appointment, but had found an interesting way of passing the time till the W7 turned up.

"Well, she *is* normally," I shrugged, ogling in wonder at my best friend's newfound brazenness.

"See that old lady standing next to them? See the look on her face?" giggled Kellie. "She'll be thinking, 'The youth of today! Tsk, tsk, tsk!'."

"Or maybe she thinks Billy caught Sandie in a swoon, and now he's giving her the kiss of life!" Salma suggested, tossing her long hair back off her face.

"What, he's giving her the kiss of life with his *tongue*?!" Kyra grimaced.

"You *are* kidding!" I squeaked in alarm at Kyra. "He is *not* using his tongue, is he?"

"Kyra's making it up! She can't see that from here!"

"Shut it, Kel! I can *so* see! I can't help it if I've got better eyesight than you!"

Kyra was grinning, enjoying winding everyone up so much that she wasn't too bothered by what was real and what wasn't. Well, maybe Billy and Sandie *weren't* kissing with tongues, but they sure were making a big show of their snogging. The way their heads were wobbling about, they'd both end up with whiplash before the W7 bus arrived...

"Y'know, whatever they're doing, it's kind of putting me off eating," Chloe said with a shudder, scrunching closed her bag of Quavers and stuffing them in her pocket.

"You're all being mean!" Jen informed us (but she still couldn't help herself smiling at what we were saying, I noticed). "They're happy! And nobody's *making* you watch, are they?"

"Morbid fascination"; that's what Grandma would have called it. Morbid fascination is that thing that makes people gawp at ambulances whooping by with their lights flashing; it's like they can't help themselves looking, like they're expecting to see blood and guts and gloop dripping out of the bottom of the ambulance door or something. And morbid fascination was the reason me and my mates were all rooted to the spot, staring at Sandie and Billy's snog-fest at the bus stop, no matter *how* gross it was.

"Jen, that is very, very true," I nodded, coming to my senses. "OK – I'm off. Catch you guys tomorrow!"

And with that, I darted off, crossing the road at the sound of the beeping Green Man and heading for home while the others couldn't seem to tear themselves – and their morbid fascination – away from the view of our friends, the snoggers.

What is it with kissing? I wondered to myself as I wandered (if you see what I mean). *It must feel good, or people wouldn't do it. But it* looks *so disgusting…*

I guess my lack of fantastic kissing experiences might have something to do with my bleak view of snogging. I'd never got that far on my two not-quite-dates with Feargal O'Leary (and since he turned out to be a jealous git, it was no great loss), and the burping-in-my-mouth incident with Keith Brownlow was about as romantic as having a hole drilled in your head. (*Please* don't ask me to go into detail.)

But if Alfie ever declared undying love (fat chance) and wanted to kiss me (even fatter chance), well, *that* might just make me change my mind, I guess…

"Hey, wait up!" a voice yelped in my ear, as a bike wheel screeched to a near stop behind me, using my leg as a kind of braking tool.

"Ouch!" I yelped back, bending down and pulling up my trouser leg to inspect the damage. Disappointingly, my leg looked its normal white, hairy self, and the only damage was a bit of a dusty tyre mark on my trousers. Hey, at least it now coordinated with my earth-encrusted black shoe, rescued from the garden this morning...

"Sorry, Al! I was just trying to catch you up!" Billy panted, reminding me for a second of Rolf. They were quite similar after all: both friendly and gangly ... and both goofballs. The only difference was that Billy wore baseball caps and Rolf was hairier (as far as I was aware).

As Billy panted – still perched on his bike – I noticed that steam was practically rising off his damp, clinging, white school shirt, thanks to him racing across Alexandra Palace to meet Sandie before she headed off to the dentist after school, and then zooming after me just now.

"Why did you want to catch me up?" I quizzed him. What I *wanted* Billy to say was something like, "'Cause I just wanted to hang out with you; see how you were doing with your mum being back and everything." But Billy is a berk, and I had a sneaking suspicion that he was going to come out with a reason that sounded altogether less thoughtful and caring.

"Sandie's bus came," he shrugged, living up (make that *down*) to my expectations.

"*Urgh...*"

"What? What did I say?"

I started walking away from Billy, forcing him to try and shove his feet back on the pedals and wobble slowly alongside me on the pavement.

"Ally?"

"Billy, don't you get it?" I half-laughed, half-frowned at him. "You make it sound like hanging out with me is a booby prize! Like, 'Sandie's gone ... I'm a bit bored ... oh, *I* know! I'll go and run over Ally to pass the time!'"

"But it's not like that! I mean ... I don't mean it to *sound* like that," Billy protested, nearly wobbling his way into someone else on the pavement (and getting a dirty look for his trouble). "I still like you! You're still my mate! It's just me and Sandie..."

"...are in *love*?" I teased him, putting on a stupid voice and fluttering my eyelashes at him.

I have never seen anyone go so bright red in my life. And that includes me.

Billy suddenly looked like he'd been force-fed a

bucket of red hot chilli peppers (the small, edible, vicious plants; not the band of the same name, *natch*). Hey, this could be fun!

"I... I *don't*... I mean... I don't ... *you* know – what you said!" Billy blustered *luminously*.

"*What* was that?" I replied, leaning closer to him and putting my hand to my ear. "Was that sentence in *English* 'cause it just sure sounded like a whole lot of *babble* to me. Maybe you should try using grammar next time!"

Ah, winding Billy up! I'd temporarily forgotten what great entertainment that was.

"I *said*, I don't ... not exactly."

"You don't 'not exactly' what?" I asked, not letting Billy off the hook for a second.

"I'm not ... I'm not in *thingy* with Sandie, OK?"

Billy was so agitated he nearly wobbled his way into a tree. I took pity on him – he was still my mate after all, and I didn't want to end up taking him to the casualty department of our local hospital. (Nurse: "So what caused Billy's crash?" Me: "Sheer embarrassment...")

"So, if you're not in *thingy* with Sandie, what *are* you?" I asked, dropping the sarcasm (reluctantly). "How *do* you feel about her?"

Billy gave up his dangerous wobbling, throwing his leg over the bike and ending up walking beside me, pushing it along. Actually, apart from avoiding damage to *himself*, other pedestrians and innocent trees, I think Billy also used it as a delaying tactic, giving him time to come up with an answer to my prying question.

"I just ... *like* her," he finally mumbled, spinning his baseball cap around so the peak of it now covered his still-blushing neck.

"Yeah, but you like *me*, and you don't want to snog my face off in front of grannies at bus stops!" I pointed out. "So it's got to be more than just *liking* her, hasn't it?"

I sneaked a sideways peek at Billy and saw him wrinkle up his (blush-tinted) nose and frown his forehead into (blush-tinted) furrows, as he struggled to put his feelings into words.

"She's..."

Uh-oh! Here it came! Maybe my berk of a best mate was going to give me the sort of insight into love and romance that would finally make sense to me.

"...I dunno. She's sort of cute. Like a little bunny or something."

So, *that* was the secret of Billy and Sandie's grand romance, in his eyes at least. Well, somehow, I *didn't* think I'd end up daydreaming my Maths lessons away from now on, imagining the wonderful moment when someone (Alfie, if miracles happened) held me close, and whispered those magic words in my ear: "Oh, Ally! You're … I dunno … *cute*, like a bunny!"

And another thing – next time Billy came round, I was going to keep him *well* away from Cilla our rabbit, just in case he got a crush on her too…

"Want a bit of this?"

"Yes, please."

Wow, I was honoured. Five seconds after I'd got in the door, and Linn was offering me some of her completely gorgeous, "Property of Linn Love" mandarin and strawberry yoghurt. (Er … I already *knew* it was gorgeous, 'cause I'd pinched a spoonful out of it last night. Hey, it was one of those big tubs, so I figured she wouldn't notice.)

Linn crashed down a matching bowl to hers in front of me and dolloped yoghurt into it.

Outside in the garden Tor (recently picked up from after-school club by Linn) and Ivy (picked up directly afterwards from Dad's shop – where Mum had left her before her hairdresser appointment – by Tor and Linn) were playing some game which involved coaxing Britney the pigeon to land on Ivy's head, using stale breadcrumbs as bait.

"Nice?" Linn asked bluntly, as I dived into the yoghurt.

"Yep," I nodded, my mouth too full of good tastes to say much more. And my head was too full of thoughts about how kind and nice Linn was underneath that layer of grouchiness to come up with much else either.

Actually, you know something mad? I was just as scared of giving Linn a compliment like that as I was of criticizing her. (I could get my head bitten off *either* way.) Good grief, what a coward I was. Here was a perfect opportunity to get stuff off my chest to Linn – to ask her about why she was being so frosty with Mum; about why she seemed so mad at Alfie the other day in Queen's Woods – but *still* I didn't have the bottle to come out with any of that.

And then the Grouch Queen spoke.

"Tor said something funny on the way home from school just now," she started up, examining her spoon for smears or stray cat hairs before she started eating her own bowl of yoghurt.

"What was that?"

Unlike Linn, I wasn't in the least bit fussy about smears and cat hairs, and had already nearly finished off my bowl before she'd begun.

"He said that he *liked* Mum, but he didn't really

feel like she *was* his mum. Which makes sense, I guess, since Tor was so young when she left. He can't really remember a time when she was here, can he?"

Overwhelmingly, two things immediately zapped into my mind:

1) It was horribly sad for both Mum and Tor if that was true; and...

2) Billy might not have given me any great insight into romance on the way home from school today, but at least he *tried* to put his feelings into words, which was more than *I* could do sometimes. But maybe I should give it a go.

"But *we* remember her being here, don't we?" I piped up. "So it's up to me and you and Rowan to explain to Tor how much fun it was having Mum around, isn't it?"

Like Billy earlier on, Linn seemed temporarily lost for words, and had that pinkified glow about her all of a sudden. What was she going to say? Had I stirred some memories? Had I made her feel a pinprick of guilt for snipping at Mum over the last couple of days?

Linn didn't get a chance to answer; a thunder of feet hammering down the stairs put paid to that, followed by a vision of denim and rainbows and Rowan and mad plaits in the kitchen doorway.

Wearing a polo neck. (Excuse me? What was with the polo neck? Wasn't it still early September and reasonably warm out there?)

"Going out for a while! Don't know how long I'll be!" Ro announced wide-eyed, before disappearing as fast as her sunflower flip-flops would take her.

There you go; a polo neck and flip-flops. If that wasn't a sign that she was a total space cadet, what was? Unless, of course...

"What's she up to?" Linn mused, leaning forward on the table and looking exactly, *exactly* like a lioness about to pounce.

I said nothing and concentrated on the yoghurt. After all, I was quite enjoying this brief interlude of Linn being almost human (part-girl/part-lioness), so what was the point of ruining everything by talking about Rowan, or bringing up the maybe/possibly love bite I'd seen on her neck last night...?

Chapter 13

ONE BIG SHOCK AND AN OUCH

Where was Rowan when you needed her? Still out doing her mystery "something" it seemed.

What a shame that she was missing out on seeing Mum before she and Dad went out tonight. One of Ro's fave pastimes is dressing up, but she gets a big kick out of seeing other people dressing up too, and Mum was looking especially nice in all her hippiefied glam-ness. (And yes, I *know* those aren't proper words, but they exactly described how Mum was looking.)

"Your hair's nice, Mum. They didn't cut off too much."

Wow, a compliment from Linn! She must have finally taken what Dad said to heart. Or maybe she just felt sorry for Mum, after what Tor had said on the way home from school...

"Thanks, Linn," Mum smiled a grateful smile. "What do you think, Ally?"

She twirled for me, letting her midnight blue, layered velvet skirt spin out. On top she wore a fitted black shirt of some fragile antique material, with tiny shiny buttons that switched from black to iridescent blue when the light caught them. Her legs were bare and on her feet she wore a pair of sweet, old-fashioned black shoes that fastened with a bar across and a button at the side.

"They're cute," I told her, pointing to her feet as she twirled to a standstill. "They look like tap shoes!"

"Yeah? I thought they looked more like something I should be doing Flamenco in!"

And with that, Mum held one hand aloft, swished a chunk of skirt with the other and did some fast-footed stomping on the living-room floorboards. She might have sent a few petrified cats running for cover, but she earned a whole bunch of clapping and whooping from me, Tor and Ivy. And of course from Dad, who'd just appeared in the doorway. He was smiling, but with a funny expression on his face, of surprise and happiness and shyness all wrapped up in one. Call me mad (and people do, regularly), but it was as if he was looking at Mum for the first time or something.

"Well... I guess... I guess that we should be going," Mum laughed nervously, acting all bashful at getting nabbed fooling around by Dad. (See? I wasn't the only one getting stupidly shy round here!)

"Let's wave!" said Tor, pulling me by the hand to the bay window, as soon as the front door clicked shut behind our parents.

Ivy didn't join us; she was too busy settling back down to play Animal Hospital with some bandages and plasters from our First Aid kit and a selection of "sickly" soft toys dragged down from Tor's room. But I was surprised when Linn joined us, watching Mum and Dad stroll off along Palace Heights Road together. Actually, on closer inspection, she *wasn't* watching Mum and Dad – she was staring in the opposite direction altogether.

"What are you looking for?" I asked, peering past our overgrown shrubs at the wide expanse of empty pavement that was holding Linn's attention.

"Alfie," Linn stated, unaware that my heart had just back-flipped at the mere mention of his name. "He's late. He's meant to be calling for me before we head off to Mary's to study together."

(Ha! Studying together... If that was anything like when me and *my* friends got together to "study", it meant that Linn would spend the next few hours talking, listening to music etc. with Alfie and Mary – followed by a frantic late-night attempt to do her homework when she got back in.)

"Do you want to play with us?" Tor suddenly

turned and suggested, just as Mum and Dad vanished out of sight around the corner.

Linn might not show the world in general that she's a nice person too often, but she does adore Tor and finds it hard to say no to him. So, along with me – for the next ten minutes till the doorbell rang – she allowed herself to be bandaged and patted by Dr Tor, while Nurse Ivy told her she was "a very good kitty".

"I'll get it!" I announced, at the shrill of the bell.

For one thing it made sense for me to go, since a) Linn had both arms bandaged to her body, which would make it difficult to get a grip on the door handle and b) well, it was an excuse to have Alfie to myself for a few brief, blissful seconds, wasn't it?

"Why have you got a plaster on your forehead?" Billy quizzed me, as soon as I pulled open the door.

And why aren't you Alfie? I wanted to ask in return, but of course didn't.

"Apparently, I'm a squirrel, and a very big nut hit me on the head," I explained, standing back to let Billy and Sandie pass.

"Ah, this is a Spook-kid thing, right?" Billy asked rhetorically, figuring out that anything to do with animals had to involve Tor.

"Don't call him Spook-kid," I told Billy for the

zillionth time, knowing that he'd just ignore me anyway. "And we're playing Animal Hospital."

"Brilliant!" smiled Sandie. "That'll be a laugh! Hello, Tor! Hello, Ivy! Can we play too?"

As Sandie bounded ahead of us into the living room, I thought about asking Billy what he was doing here, since I'd only invited Sandie round to help me babysit tonight. But it would have been a stupid question, really; I forgot the two of them were joined at the hip these days. Instead I shut up and just accepted that I'd have two friends for the price of one keeping me company tonight. Just as long as they didn't start *snogging* in front of me...

"Listen, Ally," said Linn, glancing up from the floor as she unravelled a kilometre of bandage from round her body. "If Alfie turns up, tell him I got bored waiting and went round to Mary's without him."

"Fine," I mumbled, spotting something that Linn was too preoccupied with bandages to notice. Why did Billy and Sandie swap those weird glances just there?

I had my answer a few seconds later, when Linn went out and – leaving Billy to the mercy of the kids – Sandie urged me to follow her to the kitchen.

"What?" I asked, wondering what she had to say that she *couldn't* say in front of Tor and Ivy.

"Just now, before we came round here, me and Billy were hanging out in the park," Sandie began, wide-eyed. "And you'll never guess what we saw!"

"Grass … trees … a couple of dogs, maybe…" I joked around.

"No, Ally! We saw Rowan – and Alfie!"

"*Together?!*" I heard myself asking stupidly.

"Uh-huh! They were on that bench that's half-way up the hill, and they were … *kissing*!"

It was on the tip of my tongue to ask Sandie if she was sure it was them (since she couldn't … er … get a great view of their faces if they were attached to one another), but that would have been kind of dumb. The way Rowan dressed, you'd be able to recognize her from Mars, without the aid of a telescope. And as for Alfie … Sandie knew I'd only had a crush on him since for ever, so she was pretty familiar with what he looked like too.

So instead of saying anything, I flopped down on to the nearest chair, letting my jaw drop open and my heart dissolve into pure *mush*.

"Look! Look at Billy!" Tor giggled, as he and Ivy shoved a hopping Billy in front of them into the kitchen. I don't know quite what animal they'd decided he was, but he must have had a very serious leg injury for them to have bandaged his knees together like that.

I think my kid brother and sister had hoped I'd find that funnier than I did, but right then I wouldn't have managed to crack a smile even if someone offered me a million pounds and a big tickle. What I'd just heard was simply too awesome to comprehend...

"Ally's ill!" Ivy announced, appearing by my side and mistaking my stunned expression for sickness. "Ouch!"

Ivy meant well; she really did. It's just that three and a half year olds can be a little clumsy, and when she reached across to plant a get-better plaster on my cheek, she managed to poke me in the eye with her finger while she was at it.

Still, there's nothing like the pain of a sharp poke in the eye with a small finger to take your mind off a bad shock...

Chapter 14

MADLY, SADLY...

Amazingly, it was still only Thursday night. I say amazingly, because after the news I'd just had, it felt like my brain had gone into orbit and back.

Billy and Sandie had left a while ago, Tor and Ivy had gone to bed long before (Tor snoozing among his piles of bandaged soft toys, Ivy in the middle of the big orange bed), and there was still no sign of Rowan, Linn, Mum or Dad.

As for me – if you couldn't tell already, I was still in a state of shock. (And I still had a bloodshot eye, in case you were wondering.) At least having the house (almost) to myself gave me the opportunity of lying on the sofa with a cat or two and trying to take in the news properly. After all, it wasn't every day that I found out my sister...

a) had a secret boyfriend;

b) had a secret boyfriend who'd given her a love bite;

c) had a secret boyfriend who I was madly in love with;

d) had a secret boyfriend who was the best friend of our older sister, who was going to *kill* Rowan when she found out.

You want to know how all that made me feel exactly? Well, do you remember those ancient *Roadrunner* cartoons, where Wile E Coyote always ends up falling down into endless ravines in every episode, looking faintly surprised as the dusty desert earth comes shooting up at him? Yep – that was it *exactly*.

While I lay there on the sofa going quietly demented, the cat that wasn't Colin currently lying across my chest sat bolt upright, his crossed-eyes wide and alert at a sound I couldn't quite hear yet.

"What is it, Derek?" I whispered, scratching his head while straining my own pathetically useless human ears for the mystery noise.

Then a rattle of a key in the door answered my question.

"Oh ... hi!" said a fleeting vision in the shape of Rowan, as she hurried past the living-room door and bolted up the stairs.

But Ro wasn't going to get away with it *that* easily. Without even thinking what I was going to say to her, I left the sofa to the cats and hurried after her, stumbling into her bizarre boudoir of a bedroom just as she flicked on the last ream of her many reams of fairy lights.

"Ally!" she jumped in surprise, as if the abominable snowman had just walked in on her.

"Where have you been?" I asked her, just for the fun of seeing what she said.

"What's with the plaster?" Rowan quizzed me, pointing to my forehead while ignoring my question.

"Long story. Where have you been?"

"Oooh, and your *eye*! That looks really *sore*!"

"It's OK – it looks worse than it is. So, where have you been tonight, Ro?" I persisted.

Rowan bit her lip, then seemed to be about to speak. But instead, she suddenly plonked herself down on the edge of her bed, and fell backwards, flinging her arms so wide it was as if she was gathering up the cotton roses printed on the white duvet.

"Ally ... I am *soooooo* in love!" she sighed happily.

"With?"

I tiptoed closer to the bed, curious to read her expression. Blissful. It was blissful.

"With Alfie. With ALFIE! Can you believe it?! I AM IN LOVE WITH ALFIE!"

She was sitting up again now, arms in the air this time, yelling loud enough to wake half of Crouch End.

"Rowan!" I shushed her, running over to the bed and slapping my hands around her mouth.

All that did was make her giggle, and despite all the mad feelings I'd been having all evening (or maybe *because* of them), I suddenly got the giggles too. Rolf, alerted by the yelling, stuck his snout around the bedroom door, and looked well confused by the sight of the two of us sitting in the middle of Rowan's fairy grotto, shaking with laughter, and getting louder the quieter we tried to be.

Alarmed though he was, Rolf slunk in, flopped down and dropped his puzzled head between his hairy paws as he gazed up and waited for us to come to our senses.

"So … since when?" I finally asked her, as the hysteria I was experiencing finally began to fade.

"Since when what?" asked Rowan, wiping her eyes and struggling to reign in her own giggles.

"Since when have you been in love with Alfie?"

OK, so Rowan had obviously been out with Alfie tonight. And something had obviously happened yesterday between Alfie and Rowan, after the official photographer had left them. But even if they'd suddenly, *instantly* fallen for each other over a snap or two, how could Rowan be talking about being in love already?

"Since the first time Linn ever brought him

home…" she replied dreamily. "And every day since."

Snap! I felt like saying.

"You've fancied him for *years*?" I double-checked with her instead, watching her nod happily in reply.

Wow. I had to hand it to Rowan; I'd never have expected the Princess of Blubbing to keep a secret like that for all this time. If I hadn't been in such shock, I'd have been *well* impressed.

"Oh, Ally – I've never been able to get him out of my mind. It's just … just *everything* about him!"

Tell me about it.

"There've been times when I've looked at Linn and thought, are you *mad*?! Haven't you noticed how brilliant and cool and *gorgeous* your friend is?"

Ooh, this was getting spooky … this could be *me* talking. Only it wasn't, and it wasn't *me* that Alfie had hung out with all evening. I half worried I might *faint* if I got one more surprise tonight, but there were things I urgently had to ask.

"And does Alfie feel the same way?"

"Uh-huh!" Rowan giggled some more, slapping her hands across her chest in surprised delight. "Isn't it spooky?! He's liked me for ages too, only he never did anything about it, 'cause he thought with him being a couple of years older than me there was too much of an age difference."

Too much of a *Linn* difference, more like. Linn was never, ever going to be keen on the idea of her mate dating her (annoying) younger sis. Was that why she was in such a grump in Queen's Woods the other day when she saw Alfie there? Had she sniffed out the fledgling romance between him and Ro before it had even started?

"And then he said he saw my photo in that magazine and realized I wasn't just Linn's little sister any more, and he was being really dumb to let the age thing get in the way! Isn't that brilliant?!"

Yeah, it was brilliant for Rowan; it was just rubbish for me...

"It's brilliant," I nodded at her, hoping I came across as being genuinely chuffed for her.

"And you know what he said to me tonight, Al? He said he'd *always* thought I was 'fascinating'. Can you believe it?"

Sadly yes. 'Cause there was no doubt that Rowan was fascinating, as well as being sweetly silly, irritatingly vague, amazingly original and downright wonderful. No wonder Alfie had fallen for her (and not me...).

"So ... what's happened exactly? I mean, are you and Alfie properly going out now, or what?"

"Uh-huh!" Rowan laughed, as if she couldn't quite believe it herself. "Alfie came along to take photos yesterday 'cause he thought that would be a good way to get close to me and suss out how I felt, y'know, away from the house and ... um ... and everything."

"Everything" meaning "Linn", maybe?

"And so after the photographer left, I thought Alfie might just keep taking pictures of me," Rowan continued, "but instead, he sat down next to me on this log, and we started talking, and we *kept* on talking, and that seemed unbelievably wonderful anyway. But then somehow ... somehow we ended up leaning towards each other and kissing!"

"And that's when you got the love bite?"

"Omigod!" Rowan squealed, slapping her hand on the high neck of her jumper. "You *saw* that?! When did you spot it?"

"Last night, when you came and knelt on the windowsill with me and Linn!" I told her, suddenly realizing that Rowan had probably been on the verge of telling me what had happened with Alfie then, if only she'd found me alone in my room and not hanging out with Linn and spying on Mum and Dad instead.

"Linn! She didn't see it too, did she?" Rowan asked in alarm.

"No, don't think so," I tried to reassure her. "But, hey, you do realize you can't walk around with a polo neck on all week, don't you? The weather forecast says it's going to be really warm this week!"

"I'll wear a choker! Oh, but then they won't let me wear one at school, will they?"

"Hey, *I* know," I said, coming up with an idea.

I reached up and peeled off the plaster that had been stuck to my forehead the whole evening and handed it to Ro.

"Check it out; that should be about the right size to cover it. Tell everyone that one of the cats scratched you by accident when you were cuddling it."

"Oh, Ally! You are amazing!" Rowan blinked at me in wonder. (It was quite a nice feeling, you know, having your sister blink at you in wonder. I'd have preferred Alfie to be in love with me instead of her, of course, but as a consolation prize, being told you're amazing ain't bad.)

"Whatever..." I mumbled shyly at her compliment.

"But you've got to promise me something, Ally!"

"What?"

"Promise me you won't tell Linn? Please! I've made Alfie promise!"

I could understand her panic. The wrath of Linn was a mighty terrifying prospect.

"But if you two are going out, she's going to have to know sometime!" I pointed out, my deranged brain going off on a tangent and imagining Alfie and Rowan having to meet in secret in a range of disguises; with maybe Alfie dressed as a gorilla and Rowan as a belly-dancer...

"Oh, I know she'll have to find out eventually, but—"

The sound of the front door opening stopped Ro in her tracks. Was it the Grouch Queen herself, back from her friend Mary's? Where – uh-oh – Alfie was meant to have been this evening, till love-blindness distracted him...

"Listen, Linn was supposed to be seeing Alfie tonight – you'd better phone him and tell him to come up with a good excuse for forgetting!" I hissed at Rowan.

"Hold on – it's not her; it's Mum and Dad," said Ro, tiptoeing over Rolf and positioning herself at a perfect earwigging vantage point by the slightly open door.

"What do they sound like?" I whispered, following her over. "Are they laughing? Do they sound happy?"

Rowan put a finger to her lips, and together we listened ... to silence.

And the silence dragged on, broken only by the

rustle of jackets being hung up and the click of the kettle being switched on. You know, I *really* didn't like that silence.

"Don't worry about making tea for me, Martin," we heard Mum say. "I think I'll just head for bed. 'Night…"

"Oh, right…" Dad's voice drifted in reply. "Goodnight, then, Mel."

Now excuse me if I'm wrong, but that did *not* sound to me like two people who were madly in love with each other. Unfortunately…

Chapter 15

WIDE AWAKE! ZZZZZZ...

ROMANCE – *The dictionary definition: love, esp. romantic love idealized for its purity and beauty.*
ROMANCE – *The Billy Stevenson definition: giving someone a 10p, semi-melted, white chocolate mouse.*

Well, excuse me for being cynical, but a 10p, semi-melted white chocolate mouse could *never* be described as pure and beautiful. So why had Sandie gone so slushy-gushy when Billy gave it to her? And sorry if I sounded stupid, but what *was* the secret of romance exactly...?

Urgh – for the second night in a row, I was lying in bed with a head full of thoughts thumping around so noisily in my head that I couldn't quite sleep. Since I wasn't in the mood for reading, and listening to music was out (Winslet ate my headphones), I decided to dig out my little inspiration journal and doodle down some thoughts on romance, just to see if putting stuff on paper made any more sense than it did in my head.

Here's the main thing that I couldn't understand about love and romance and all that gubbins... *How come* Billy and Sandie were together, after years of liking each other about as much as measles, and *how come* Rowan and Alfie were now an instant item, after years of hiding how much they liked each other, and yet Mum and Dad – who'd loved each other for years and years and years and had five kids to prove it – couldn't seem to hit it off together at all? Maybe Dad was missing the point and should have given Mum a chocolate mouse instead of treating her to a posh meal tonight...

But my scribbles didn't help at all. After staring at them stupidly for a while, I knew there was only one thing for it: biscuits. (The amount of late-night kitchen raids *I* was going on, they'd have to widen my bedroom door to let me out of it soon...)

It really was late, with every light switched off and the sound of sleep seeping out of every bedroom as I made my way downstairs. Padding along the hallway towards the kitchen, though, I could make out a small glow of something. Maybe it was the oven light – everyone in our family tended to forget to flick that off, much to the annoyance of Grandma, who was always moaning on about what a waste of electricity it was and making us feel as guilty as if we'd personally punched that hole in the ozone layer.

But there was more than just that glow coming from the kitchen … there was also a soft flow of air wafting through, carrying the scent of the jasmine bush that overhung our bins. Had the cat flap popped out again? That happened last week when Rolf had tried to follow Colin through the flap – forgetting he was a large dog and not a small moggy. After a bit of a tussle, Rolf had ended up wearing the plastic cat flap round his neck, leaving a great big breezy hole in the bottom of the back door.

But no … the cat flap was intact and the oven light was safely turned off (Grandma would be pleased to note). Instead I spotted – with my heart doing a loop-de-loop – that the back door was standing wide open, and a figure was crouched down on the step. My first instinct was BURGLARRR! HELLLPPP!! but then I realized that the average burglar doesn't sit with an aromatherapy candle burning beside them, and no matter how useless Rolf was as a guard dog, he wouldn't sit still and let his ears get scratched by an arch criminal.

"Hi! Who's that?" Mum turned and asked, peering through the dark kitchen to see who'd just stood on the creaky floorboard (or maybe she'd just heard my heart thumping).

"It's me … it's Ally," I replied, padding over towards Mum so that she could see me better in the candlelight.

"Couldn't sleep, babes?" she asked, pulling Rolf over towards her a little and making space for me to join her on the steps.

"Nope," I replied, folding myself up and crouching myself down, like an origami girl in pyjamas. (The back door wasn't that wide – it was a tight squeeze to fit a mum, a dog and an Ally in there. Specially an Ally that had been eating too many midnight snacks lately…)

"What's on your mind? Anything in particular stopping you sleep?"

Even in this half-light, Mum looked so pretty close up, her hair all loose and wavy around her face, her green eyes deep and translucent as she smiled at me. Now was my chance; it was just me and her (and Rolf). I'd just ask her straight out, ask her what had happened with Dad tonight at the restaurant.

And then, uh-oh … here came another maddening wave of shyness, paralysing my brain and my throat so that all the questions I wanted to ask her got stuck down a dead-end street somewhere deep inside my head. But Mum was still looking directly at me, waiting for an answer, so I had to say *something*.

"There's this boy I really like…" I began.

"OK," Mum nodded. "So what's the deal with the boy?"

"The deal is, I just found out tonight that he's going out with … a girl I know."

I didn't think I could bring myself to tell her that the boy was Alfie and the girl was Rowan. Even though Rowan and me had had that weird, hysterical fit of the giggles together earlier, I was back to feeling like a real loser about the whole thing now.

"Hmm … *that's* got to hurt," Mum muttered, staring off out into the darkened garden. "Did he *know* you liked him?"

"No. I never told him. I didn't suppose he'd be interested in me. And he wasn't, *obviously*…"

"Well, I don't know this boy, but if you liked him so much, he must have been nice. You've got good taste, Ally."

I felt a warm flush at her compliment. Lucky there was only the little candle for light or she'd have been marvelling at my amazing, blushable cheeks close up.

"And there's nothing I can say to make you feel any better at the moment," Mum continued, "but the only bit of advice I'd give you for the future is that if there *is* a boy you like, you should try and let him know."

"What – tell someone you like them, just like that?" I asked, feeling my toes curl at the idea of a boy laughing in my face in response.

"No, not by telling him out loud, necessarily – just by talking to him and having a laugh with him. It's just that people aren't psychic, you know. You could let someone slip through your fingers 'cause they didn't have a clue you liked them. And that would be a real shame, wouldn't it?"

Mum was more right than she knew, in a completely different way; Alfie and Rowan had wasted such a lot of time, both fancying each other but acting as if they didn't. Good grief – Rowan could have been his girlfriend ages ago, saving me years and years of useless, unrequited drooling...

And you know something else Mum was right about? Alfie fancying Rowan in the first place. She'd spotted the signs the other day, only I didn't believe her at the time. (Stupid, dumb me.)

"Hey, look at you yawning!" Mum laughed softly. "I think you'd better get yourself back to bed, young lady!"

"Maybe," I mumbled through another yawn, feeling suddenly, *totally* exhausted.

As I scrambled to my feet, I thought about leaning across and hugging her, or kissing her on the cheek, like I used to do (a long, long time ago…). But guess what? Yes – I bottled it.

"'Night, then," I whispered, as I headed over to the kitchen door and out into the hallway.

"'Night, Ally Pally!" Mum smiled at me from the step, all lit up in soft focus by candlelight.

For a second, in my tiredness, I felt like I had just dreamt her up; that in the morning I'd wake, come down here to the kitchen and there'd just be the five of us – me, Dad, Linn, Rowan and Tor. It would be like Mum and Ivy had never been here.

What a weird thought.

I really *did* need my sleep…

Chapter 16

HELLO, MR PENGUIN!

Out of the corner of my eye, I could see Ivy sidling up beside me at the kitchen table.

She took her time, stepping, then stopping, then stepping some more, till she was a little pink presence right by my elbow.

"This is Mr Penguin," she whispered, as if she was letting me in on a very special secret.

"Hello, Mr Penguin," I said, directly to Tor's favourite soft toy, which Ivy was clutching very tenderly. "Would you like a bit of my toast?"

Ivy shook her head hard.

"Don't eat toast," she muttered, slapping a small hand across Mr Penguin's mouth.

I presumed she meant 'cause he was a penguin, and only ate fish or something. I presumed wrong.

"Why not?" I checked with her.

"He's a *toy*," she told me matter-of-factly.

"I see…" I nodded, hoping I could keep a straight face.

(Funny how it hadn't mattered that the toys were

just, er, *toys* last night when she was playing Animal Hospital and fixing their broken beaks or whatever.)

"Tor's given Ivy Mr Penguin to keep!" Mum informed me, as she bent over to grab a few breakfast plates that were finished with.

"It's OK, let me," said Linn, grabbing the plates up first and managing a bit of a smile in Mum's direction. (Dad – busy slurping coffee out of his mug – pretended not to register that effort on Linn's part, but I clocked him taking it in.)

"Mr Penguin is to make up for missing ... B-E-N," Rowan spelt out for me from the other side of the table.

"Oh..." I nodded back, as Mr Penguin started taking a walk up my arm.

Tor – in the garden shed doing a last-minute-before-leaving-for-school check on Branston the poorly gerbil – was missing out on this. Which was a pity really, 'cause it was almost normal and almost wonderful, having my whole family here, sharing a silly conversation over tea and toast and toy penguins. Yep, my paranoid half-waking nightmare hadn't come true last night... I'd come down to breakfast this morning to find Mum and Ivy most definitely still here (thank goodness). And Mum and Dad seemed to be getting on all right, despite the silence me and Ro had overheard last night (thank goodness again). In fact, we were all getting on just fine (thank goodness times three).

Er, who said anything about speaking too soon?

"*Hmmm, hmm, hmmm, hmm, hmmm, up a tree! K-I-S-S-I-N-G!*" Ivy sing-songed happily, as she stretched up on to her bunny-suited tiptoes and bounced Mr Penguin up on to my shoulder.

"*Who's* kissing *who* up the tree?" I grinned at her, raising my eyebrows at her conspiratorially.

I had expected her to say something like Rolf and Colin. I hadn't expected her to point at Rowan, giggle, and say, "an' Alfie!"

Good *grief*.

And it didn't look like Rowan or Linn expected that either.

Maybe it's just the way my befuddled head works, but suddenly everything started to move in slow motion, with Linn stopping in mid-tidy and letting one crumb-covered plate clatter noisily back on to the table.

"Oops!" said Mum, reaching forward and scooping it – and another teetering plate from Linn's hands – as Linn fixed Rowan with a this-better-not-be-true glower.

"Hey, that sounds a bit silly!" Dad grinned at Ivy, his words booming out like I was hearing them from down a long tunnel. "Who said that?"

"Andie!" Ivy trilled, while walking Mr Penguin back down my arm.

"Andie?" Dad repeated, confused.

Oh no, oh no, oh *noooooo*...

"*Sandie*?!" I saw Linn turn and hiss at me in confusion.

Oh, please, *please* don't say Ivy and Tor heard what Sandie told me last night in the kitchen...

"Hold on." Dad frowned. "Ivy, *Sandie* said something to you? About *Rowan* and Alfie?"

Ivy nodded her head. "Kissin' Hee, hee, heee!" she giggled, snuggling Mr Penguin up to my face for a smooch. (Y'know, funnily enough, I wasn't in the mood to smooch him back just then.)

"Well, I think Sandie was maybe just saying that for a joke," Dad shrugged jovially at Ivy. "Rowan hasn't kissed Alfie! Have you, Ro?"

And there I was thinking I'd never seen anyone go as red as Billy the other day, when he denied being in "thingy" with Sandie. Wrong! Rowan's poor little face went from pink, to fuchsia, to crimson, to tomato in three-quarters of a second flat. I think everyone could take that as an admission of guilt.

"You've snogged *Alfie*?" Linn roared her lioness roar, practically sending Rowan's plaits flying in the accompanying blast of air. "I *knew* something was going on! How could you *do* this! He's *my* friend! Couldn't you have found someone *else* to snog? Why did you have to snog MY BEST FRIEND!"

Me and my sisters try never to lose it in front of Dad, but it's safe to say that Linn had most definitely lost it. And while Mum, Dad and Ivy looked shocked (and Rowan looked plain terrified), I suddenly understood where Linn was coming from. It was exactly the same situation as me and Billy and Sandie. It wasn't so much that I resented them being in love (or in "thingy", or whatever), I just resented the fact my two best friends spent so much time together that they often forgot about me.

In that flash of a second, I understood that *that's* what was bugging Linn: the idea of losing her best friend, and instead imagining him hanging around our house as usual, only not with *her*. I felt hugely sorry for Linn right then, and – hey – even if she didn't know it, and even if it *was* for totally different reasons, we had something in common; neither me or Linn were too delirious about the idea of Rowan and Alfie being girlfriend and boyfriend.

"Look, let's all calm down," Mum muttered, reaching over to put her arm around Linn.

Just as she did that, Mum's eyes met mine for a

moment, and – it could have been my befuddled brain playing tricks with me again – I had the oddest, most uncomfortable feeling that she was reading my mind. Urgh ... drinking a tumbler full of vinegar couldn't make my insides curl up with embarrassment as much as they were doing right that *second*.

"Get off me, Mum!" Linn barked, shrugging Mum's comforting arm away. "You can't come swanning back here after all this time and pretend to know how we're all feeling!"

And now everything swung from being in slow motion to moving at hyper-speed, with Linn vanishing out of the kitchen, grabbing her school-bag and slamming the front door shut in record-breaking time.

"What's wrong?" Tor asked, walking back dazed and confused into the emotional minefield that was our kitchen.

"Nothing. Time to walk you to school!" Mum said brightly, cheerfully shooing Tor and Ivy (even though she was still in her jim-jams) out of the kitchen.

"Melanie? Are you OK?" Dad called out, following them out into the hall.

"I'm fine! It's fine! Honestly!" I heard Mum assure him, as she rattled the leads for the dogs.

"Do you want to wear my wellies?" I heard Tor ask Ivy, above the din of Rolf and Winslet going barking crazy with the excitement of walkies.

"Yes, pease!" Ivy squealed back, the way other little girls get excited about trying on a tutu.

So ... while the smaller Love children happily skipped to school (Tor in his uniform, Ivy in her bunny-suit jim-jams and Tor's wellies), us older Love children would be doing much the same thing, minus the skipping and wellies and happiness part.

Linn certainly wouldn't be happy, stomping her way to school right now, growling at anyone who happened to get in her way.

As for me, well, sitting across the table was a soggy pile of girl and plaits, and I wasn't sure quite how I was going to get her out of the *kitchen*, never mind steer her along the road and get her into her first lesson of the day.

"Oh, Ally!" sniffled the Princess of Blubbing, sending trails of mascara cascading down her face. "What am I going to do?"

Why ask me? My brain had just melted. Ro would have been better off asking Mr Penguin for advice...

Chapter 17

GOING, GOING, GONE...

It came to me like a blinding flash, in Chemistry. (Don't worry, I didn't blow anything up.)

Why hadn't it entered my dumb little brain before? The *one* thing I could do to make Mum feel extra-welcome at home (specially after Linn flipped out at her this morning) was to let her read all the journals I'd kept. After all, I'd written them with *her* in mind; ten fat notebooks – eleven if you count the one about last Christmas – packed full of stories about all the funny, silly, sad and mad stuff that had happened to our family while she'd been gone. I wrote them so that *if* she came back home to us, she could catch up on everything, and not feel left out.

Well, there was no "if" about it – Mum *had* come back home, and it was about time I plonked those journals in her lap...

"Is he coming to meet you, then?"

"No," Sandie replied to Kyra's question, as the three of us ambled out of the last class of the day this Friday afternoon, me with my head full of thoughts about journals, Kyra and Sandie rabbiting on about Billy.

"Why not? Has he chucked you?" Kyra asked casually.

Sandie pursed her rosebud lips indignantly and glowered at Kyra. Actually, Sandie's too sweet to glower – it was more of a bunny-in-the-headlights startled glance, which only made Kyra grin all the more, knowing that her teasing had hit home.

"He has *not* chucked me, Kyra! He's playing football after school today! And *look* –"

Sandie pulled her pink polka-dot mobile out of her pocket and shoved it two millimetres from Kyra's nose.

"– see? He texted me! So there!"

"'*Miss yooo, xxxx yooo*'," Kyra read out, pulling her neck back so she could focus on the tiny screen properly. "Yuck! Pass the sick bucket now!"

"Kyra! You can be *so* horrible!" Sandie moaned, blinking her blue eyes furiously.

"You mean, she can be *so* good at winding you up," I corrected Sandie, trying to defuse the situation before Kyra pushed it too far and Sandie got upset. I'd had enough of people falling out with each other today, thank you very much.

"Oh, Ally! Just the girl!"

My head spun round at the sound of Miss Thomson's voice. Being the naturally talented worrier that I am, my mind immediately whirred through all the possible reasons why my favourite teacher would want to talk to me:

a) I'd completely forgotten to hand in some History homework. (Definitely possible; I'd done it before.)

b) She was passing on a message from my Maths teacher, Mr Horace, letting me know that he saw me nodding off in his class earlier. (Very possible; I'd done that before too.)

c) She'd just spotted that I had my skirt tucked in my knickers. (Unlikely, since I was wearing trousers.)

But no, it didn't seem that Miss Thomson wanted to speak to me for any of those reasons.

"Have you seen this yet, Ally? I picked up a copy at lunchtime..."

Miss Thomson had reached in her bag and pulled out a copy of the local paper. Curiosity getting the better of them, Kyra and Sandie huddled either side of me as our teacher held it open at pages two and three.

"Wow, she looks so pretty!" Sandie gasped, staring at Rowan's photo, which was huge (but not as huge as the picture of the burst sewage pipe on the page opposite, but I guess that's local papers for you).

"Yeah, she *does* look really pretty – no wonder Alfie fancies her!" Kyra commented wickedly in my left ear.

Honestly, sometimes I wonder why I'm friends with that girl. Hadn't I spent lunchtime in the park with her and Sandie today, with the two of them sympathizing over crisps and Coke about the whole heartbreaking situation with my sister and Alfie? But sympathetic or not at the time, Kyra couldn't resist having a dig when she got the chance. It's just in her nature, I guess, like it's mine to ignore her when she's annoying me...

"I wonder if Rowan's seen this yet?" I mused, skimming through the story written underneath. Even if she had, chances were Rowan wouldn't have been able to read it, considering her eyes were probably still swollen shut after her blub-a-thon over breakfast. (Poor Ro was still sniffling when I pointed her in the direction of her art class at the sound of the first bell this morning.)

"Oh, I think she has," Miss Thomson nodded. "I've just come from the staff room, and I spotted her out of the window, standing looking at a paper with some blond-haired boy who was waiting for her by the school gates."

"Alfie?" muttered Sandie softly, her mind in synch with mine.

It was bound to be, I thought dismally, feeling that familiar jab of disappointment stabbing at my dented heart...

Linn didn't bother with pleasantries like "Hello" or "Hi" or "How's your day been?" when I ran and caught up with her on the way home from school. She just launched straight into what was on her mind.

"I saw Alfie and Rowan together, when I came out of the sixth-form block."

They were nowhere in sight when me, Kyra and Sandie had left, with the copy of the paper Miss Thomson had kindly given to me.

"Did they see you?" I asked her.

"No."

I didn't say anything for a second. It was all I could do to keep up with her high-speed, anger-fuelled stride.

"Has she told *you* anything?" Linn then asked me straight out, practically spitting out the word "she".

"Only that they're ... um ... going out," I shrugged, deciding it was best not to spill the whole of Ro's confession to Linn. All the gory details would probably just wind her up even more than she was already.

"Oh, *great*. So it wasn't just a one-off snog," Linn grumbled darkly. "What a coward!"

"Excuse me?" I checked with her, not sure what she was on about.

"Well, Rowan – I wouldn't expect her to tell me anything. But Alfie – he's supposed to be my best mate and instead he's just a coward!" Linn ranted. "I phoned him this morning on the way to sixth-form, but he hasn't had the decency to call me back and tell me to my face what's going on with him and … *her*!"

Linn suddenly held up the mobile she was clutching in her hand, as if she was proving to me there wasn't a message in sight.

"I mean, what's his problem?" she ranted on. "Apart from having no *taste*, if he wants to go out with Rowan, of course. It's like, why make it such a secret? I'm his best mate! Best mates aren't supposed to have secrets from each other, are they?"

"Are you worried that you won't be friends any more?" I asked her tentatively, half-expecting a growl of a denial.

Linn seemed to be thinking that over (or maybe she was just silently mulling over ways to disembowel Rowan and Alfie).

"You know, that's *it*, Ally. That's *exactly* it," she stated, still looking frighteningly annoyed. "I'm going to phone Nadia and tell her that when we get home. She said today that maybe I'm hacked off because deep down I fancy Alfie. Can you believe it? First, I can't trust *him* to be my friend and be honest with me, and then I can't trust Nadia to understand me or take my side!"

Since we seemed to be having this sisterly sharing moment (practically a once-in-a-lifetime event with me and Linn), I thought I'd maybe tell her about Kyra, about how useless a mate she can be, but – as we approached our house – I realized Linn wasn't finished with her ranting.

"How dare Nadia tell me what I'm thinking! It was the same with Mum this morning – I didn't mean to snap at her like that, but honestly, Al, it just really bugged me the way she tried to act like … I dunno … a *mum*, I suppose, after not bothering to be around all this time!"

Who knows how long Linn planned to rave on, but since we were now at our front gate, I thought it would be a tremendously good idea if I changed the subject away from Mum and got her to shut up. I had no idea how Linn and Mum were going to respond to each other after this morning's blow-out, but I had a feeling it would make things easier if Linn *wasn't* caught whingeing about her as we walked through the door...

"Listen, I know you're working tomorrow, but do you fancy taking Tor and Ivy to the movies on Sunday?" I chattered (fake) brightly, as we walked into the house and were met by the usual welcome-home barking committee of Rolf and Winslet. "That new Walt Disney film's out this weekend and..."

I droned to a stop, realizing that the house was spookily empty of humans.

"Did Mum say if she was going out with Tor and Ivy this afternoon?" I asked an uninterested Linn, who was dropping her schoolbag with a thump on to the kitchen floor.

"Don't know. Wasn't in the mood to listen," she mumbled. "But, hey, look – I think she's left a note."

Linn was pointing to the kitchen table, where a sheet of white paper was half jutting out from underneath a purring cat that wasn't Colin.

I patted Eddie on the head, and pulled the note out from under him, without disturbing him too much.

"*'To whoever gets home first...'*" I read at the top of the page, "*'...Tor's round at Freddie's house – I arranged it with Freddie's mum this morning.'*"

"And that's it?" asked Linn, clattering the kettle under the tap.

"Yeah," I shrugged, "apart from she's signed it, *'Lots of love and sorry, Mum xxxx.'*"

It was slow motion time again, as the ominous meaning behind that small "sorry" crept into my mind. I tilted my head up, and saw from the look of alarm on Linn's face that she thought something *definitely* wasn't right here.

"Ally – go and collect Tor, now. I'm going to phone Dad!"

If Linn hadn't been there, I'd have probably flapped around, not knowing what to do or what to panic about first.

But Linn *was* there. And in moments of crisis, it's very, *very* useful to have a bossy sister around to tell you what to do...

Chapter 18

DREAMS DO COME TRUE (WORSE LUCK)

It was Tor that found the second note, propped up on the mantelpiece in-between two of Mum's handmade sculptures.

On the walk home from Freddie's we'd passed the time with me telling him wall-to-wall bad jokes ("What's orange and sounds like a parrot? A carrot!") and him laughing his head off. Well, there was no point in worrying him till we all got together with Dad and tried to work out what exactly we *were* going to worry about.

So, while me, Dad and Linn had hushed discussions in the kitchen, Tor bumbled through to the living room to play with whichever random pets wanted to be played with.

"Found this..." he piped up, rejoining us in the kitchen and handing Dad a note addressed to "Martin", in Mum's handwriting. "Where's Ivy? Where's Mum?"

"Er, dunno..." I mumbled truthfully, as I bit my lip and stared at Dad's face for clues, now that his troubled eyes were scanning Mum's words.

"They've gone, haven't they?"

Spook-kid strikes again. Y'know, Tor's always been a smart kid, sussing stuff out before we even tell him.

Dad glanced up over the note and nodded sorrowfully at Tor. And now that there didn't seem any point in shielding any of us from the truth, Dad let his eyes dart back to the note and read it out loud.

"'Martin – I can't stay. You and the girls have all moved on without me, and that's just the way it should be. I've been gone so long that I'm just an intrusion in everyone's lives. I know you won't want to admit it, but it's true, isn't it?'"

Dad stopped for a second, wincing, as if the paper he was holding was sending tiny pinpricks of shock through his fingers.

"'That's why I decided that it was best for me and Ivy to go back home to Cornwall. Tell the girls and Tor I'm so, so, sorry to leave this way... I just thought it would make it a little easier for them somehow. Love to all of you, always, Melanie.'"

"She's gone?!" Rowan squeaked in the doorway, having come in without anyone hearing her. (Even Rolf and Winslet had sensed our mood and were lying flat on the kitchen floor, their eyes soulfully staring up at us, their barking on hold.)

"Maybe Ivy missed Ben too much..." said Tor, shuffling forward and slipping his hand into mine.

Suddenly I imagined Ivy happily introducing Mr Penguin to her Golden Retriever. What about Rolf and Winslet and the cats? What about Branston the sickly gerbil, and the mice, and the stick insects she'd learned all the names of? Would she miss them now? Would she miss *us*? I gulped at the very thought of her, giving Tor's hand a squeeze that was probably a bit too hard, but he didn't complain.

"But Mum can't have gone!" Rowan croaked tearfully, still transfixed in the kitchen doorway. "I've got lots of stuff to tell her! And I was going to show her this!"

Ro was holding up the local paper, opened at her photo. I know it might have sounded trivial, but it was just the way Rowan comes out with things sometimes. After all, stress affects people in different ways, and all the sequins and fluff in Rowan's head had just been *seriously* shaken up.

"Oh, grow up, Ro!" Linn blasted at her (Linn's way of dealing with stress is to roar, after all). "How can you be so petty? Mum's gone, and all you care about is that stupid picture of yourself!"

"She *wouldn't* have gone," Rowan snapped back, her mascara on the run once more, "if you hadn't been so mean to her this morning, Linn!"

And maybe Mum wouldn't have gone, I thought to myself, blanking out my sisters' continuing slanging match, *if I'd only shown her my journals days ago, when she first arrived.*

If Mum had had a chance to read them, she'd know how much we'd all missed her over the past four years; how much we wanted her home, and how much we cared, even if some of us weren't very good at showing it.

While me and my sisters carried on beating ourselves (and each other) up about why Mum had left, Tor asked Dad a straightforward question, boy-to-man.

"What are we going to do, Dad?"

Dad ruffled his hands agitatedly through his hair and stared hard at the table, before finally coming up with something.

"Linn! Rowan!" he boomed loudly, getting their attention and making them cease fire.

He stared round at us all, one by one.

"Right," he said in a quieter, calmer voice. "Everyone, grab your toothbrushes – we're going on a trip..."

Chapter 19

MISSION: FIND MUM

"Fish...!" Rowan ruminated, scrunching her nose up.

A couple of tourists in anoraks with matching cameras slung around their necks did a double-take at her as she spoke. St Ives seemed packed full of bright colours and quirky quaintness, but a girl with a Winnie-the-Pooh plaster on her neck, dressed in a pink crochet beanie hat, a T-shirt with Ganesh the Hindu elephant god printed on it, a pair of bright red flared cords and yellow flip-flops with sunflowers on them muttering "Fish...!" was still a bit of a curiosity.

I tell you, my sister is such an oddball. Rowan had spent the last eighteen hours blubbing – and I'm counting sleeping hours too, 'cause I *swear* Ro was blubbing while she dozed – yet she still managed to dress herself like she was off to a fashion show for freaks, and not a street-by-street search for a missing mum. And now ... now she was thinking about *food*?!

"Ro, if you'd eaten breakfast, you wouldn't be

hungry," I told her, realizing five seconds later that I sounded *exactly* like Grandma.

Though Rowan didn't seem to think so; she turned and stared at me as if I'd just come out with a sentence in word-perfect Peruvian.

"What are you on about, Ally?" she asked in total bemusement.

"Well, what are *you* on about?" I countered. "It's only half-ten in the morning and you're burbling on about *fish*!"

"It was just that I thought it's a funny name for a road, that's all!"

Glancing up at where Ro was pointing, I saw the sign "Fish Street" fixed on the corner of an old building. Ahhh, yes … St Ives *did* seem to be packed with odd-sounding place names. If we were on holiday – and not on a mission – it could have been fun to go looking for the most bonkers street name in this town.

"Anyway, I didn't see *you* eating breakfast this morning, Ally," Rowan carried on, straightening her beanie hat in the reflection of a shop window. "Probably because it was disgusting."

That was saying something, coming from a girl who loves the sort of weird food combinations that only a starving vulture with its taste buds surgically removed might like too. But this one time we were agreed; breakfast at the Windy Ways B&B *was* disgusting, mainly because it consisted of a plate of grease with the occasional speck of bacon and egg floating in it. Yum (*not*).

Given a choice, I don't think the Windy Ways B&B would have been the sort of place my dad would have picked out for us to stay in. It wasn't just the non-delicious, non-nutritious breakfasts; it was also the fact that everyone else staying there seemed to be over ninety, and stared at me and my sisters and Tor as if we were aliens, or lepers, or alien lepers or something. Isn't it funny that there are old people like that? Don't they have kids, or grandkids? Has it slipped their minds that they were once kids themselves?

Whatever, Dad didn't have much of a choice, considering that he had about five seconds to phone the tourist office in St Ives and organize accommodation for us yesterday before we all hurtled across town to Paddington Station to catch the last train of the day headed for Cornwall. By the time we got there, it was too late to do any searching for Mum; all we could do was climb up the long steep road to Windy Ways, and collapse into our creaky, flouncy, frill-covered beds.

Not that any of us got much rest, what with worrying about how we'd get on today: whether we'd find Mum or not; what we'd all say and do if we *did* find her. Apart from that, it was pretty hard-going sharing a room with two sisters who weren't speaking (no matter what was going on with Mum, the Alfie business had caused a rift as wide as the *Thames* between Linn and Ro). And then, of course, Rowan was doing that sleep-blubbing thing, while Linn lay tossing and turning and *sighing* the whole night. There was plenty of sleep deprivation going on next door in Dad and Tor's room too... Tor kept Dad up for hours, lying awake and fretting that our neighbour Michael the vet – who'd kindly offered to feed the pet tribe for us – might have got muddled and missed someone out of the food chain, or fed Pedigree Chum to the tortoise and bird seed to the stick insects or whatever.

So, this morning, the Love clan (or part of it), hit the town with bleary eyes and rumbling stomachs, determined to turn detective and track down Mum and Ivy. But there were just a *couple* of little snags to our plan: 1) we didn't know where they lived; and 2) none of us could remember the name of the craft shop Mum worked in...

"It shouldn't be *too* difficult – it's only a small town," said Dad, before we started ambling around and found that this small town consisted of about a trillion arty-crafty shops. That's when Linn got usefully bossy and announced that we should split up into search parties, armed with a tourist map each, and ask around as many craft shops as we could.

"Dad, you're on your own," she'd ordered. "Tor's coming with me, and Ally – you go with … *her*. Then we'll all meet up at the pier at eleven and see who's found out what."

Well, I hoped Dad or Linn and Tor were getting on better than me and "her" (Linn seemed to find it impossible to call Rowan by her name at the moment without gagging). So far, all me and Ro had found out was that there were lots of hunky surfboarders in St Ives, and that the townspeople had named a road in honour of fish.

The problem was, a bad case of collywobbles had overcome the two of us, and we hadn't worked up the nerve to go in to any of the craft and gift shops in our Linn-appointed area of the town. The way Rowan saw it, she was positive she'd recognize the name of Mum's shop as soon as she set eyes on it – and although I severely doubted that, I was too much of a chicken to do anything else but go along with my dingbat of a sister for once.

"Gotcha…!" Rowan suddenly called out, causing the anoraked tourists to turn back and stare at her.

"'Gotcha'?" I frowned, looking around for more

dodgy street names. "There's actually a '*Gotcha* Street' here?"

"No! Over there! It's Mum's shop, I'm sure!" squealed Rowan, pointing to the small, white-washed building with "Seabird Ceramics" painted on to a wooden board above the window. Both of us stepped closer and I saw that the window contained a display overspilling with handmade pots and ornaments, trinkets and baubles.

To me, the shop name didn't sound particularly familiar, but there was no mistaking that fired clay blob in the window. Some people might have wondered who'd want to make – let alone try to *sell* – a ceramic potato with whiskers, but those with more vision would understand that it was *supposed* to be a seal. If my mother wasn't the artist responsible for that artwork, then *I* was a potato.

In a flurry of colour, Rowan vanished inside. Just as I was about to follow her, that irritating, now-familiar wave of shyness hit me like a tidal wave, and no matter how much I tried to move, my legs felt full of a strange mix of lead and jelly.

Luckily, me and my strangely afflicted legs only had to wait a minute or two to find out what was going on.

"Mum *does* work there, but she's not there

today. There's just a Saturday girl on at the moment – she doesn't know where Mum lives. But she says Mum's friend Val will be in after lunch, if we want to come back and ask her stuff then," Ro explained, talking at about a million miles an hour.

OK, so we were one (jelly-legged) step and a couple of hours closer to Mum...

It's very hard to know what to have for lunch when: a) you've had no breakfast (or at least, not one that was edible); and b) you're too excited to eat.

"Look, you guys have to eat *something*," Dad had insisted, when we'd arrived at Porthmear beach, after meandering there once we'd met up at the pier.

He was right, of course. We had to eat *something*. So we settled on ice-cream.

"What time is it now?" Tor quizzed me once he'd finished the Flake in his 99 cone.

"Five minutes later than it was last time you asked," I told him.

Spread out in front of us was a stunning view of sea, sand and surfers. But no matter how great the scenery, all this waiting around was torture. We still had another hour's worth of hanging around to do before Val would be back at the craft shop, and we were all failing miserably to kill time in our own way. Dad was staring at a paper he'd bought, but he might as well have been holding it upside down for all the attention he was paying to what was written in it. Linn was lying on her back, trickling sand through her fingers and sighing a lot. Rowan was gazing at the surfer boys as they plunged into the waves, but instead of drooling, she looked troubled, as if her mind was on Mum or Alfie or both. I couldn't concentrate on the cute surfer boys either (what a waste!), and had given up counting seagulls 'cause they kept swooping and wouldn't stay still. With the hand that wasn't holding his ice-cream, Tor had tried drawing in the sand with a stick, but he only got halfway through the outline of the stegosaurus before he gave up and flopped down beside me. Surely he wasn't going to ask me the time *again*?

"Ally..."

"Tor – I *told* you the time twenty seconds ago!" I told him, not sure whether to laugh or strangle him. (Hey, we were all feeling pretty stressed.)

"Not *that*," Tor shook his head, as he stared off into the distance. "*That!* That dog there, Ally – it's Ben!"

Dad snapped his paper shut, Linn sat bolt upright, (shedding sand everywhere), Rowan blinked out of her reverie, and I opened and shut my mouth like a hyperventilating goldfish. But Tor wasn't around to see any of this; he'd already starting running towards the Golden Retriever that was happily barking dementedly at the waves.

"BEN!" we heard Tor yell.

"It could be any dog; retrievers are really popular..." Linn muttered, her eyes fixed on our little brother.

"WOOF!" the Golden Retriever stopped suddenly and barked in reply to his name being called.

It *was* him. It *had* to be. And if that was Ben, then...

"Where are they?" I asked, panic mounting in my chest and fuzzing my vision as I cast my eyes around the strolling, milling figures on the crowded beach.

"There! That's her pink sunhat!"

It seemed that Tor wasn't the only world-class sprinter in the family; Dad had thrown aside his paper and taken off across the sand before Rowan had even finished pointing out the faraway figures of the woman and the little girl all dressed in pink, strolling through the shallows.

And then the three of us – me and Linn and Rowan – were running too, jackets and bags left behind, thundering across the shifting sands towards the mirage of Mum and Ivy. Ahead of us, Mum was already caught up in Dad's arms as he spun her around, her head tossed back as she laughed with happiness, her hair furling out in a blonde cascade behind her.

And as for us? Ivy started jumping and clapping and shrieking when she spotted me, Ro and Linn racing her way at high speed. But before either me or my sisters had a chance to scoop her up, Tor had already beaten us to it, hugging his kid sis as Ben barked and bounded excitedly around them.

And before anyone knew how it happened, all seven of us (eight, counting Ben) became one giggling, hugging, salt-water-splashed bundle of happiness and Love...

Chapter 20

WAY TOO MUCH WONDERFULNESS...

If you dream about your teeth falling out, apparently it means that there's a problem in your life that you don't know how to deal with (it says in Rowan's *Understand Your Dreams* book).

It even tells you what it means if you dream about sheds, pyjamas, cacti or *buffalo*, for goodness' sake. This is all very well, but nowhere in Ro's book does it explain what it means when you dream about being attacked by a *hoover*, which is exactly what was zapping around my subconscious last night as I slept on the floor of Mum's flat.

After a week of disturbed nights, you'd think I'd have been out like a light, all relaxed 'cause of my whole family being back together and everything being too stupidly fantastic for words. But I guess maybe I was just so excited that my feeble mind couldn't cope with all that happiness at once. Or maybe my sleep was disturbed because me and my sisters and brother (and Ben) were all camped out in Mum's living room, and the giggles and elbows and wagging tail in my face were responsible for The Attack Of The Deadly Hoover nightmare.

Oh well; what was the point in worrying about it. There was *way* too much wonderfulness going on to waste time analysing my bizarre-o dreams...

"Well, cheers, everyone!" laughed Stanley, holding up his mug of tea to us all.

"Cheers!" we all called out, untidily overlapping our voices in reply, and holding up our own mugs of tea or glasses of juice.

You know, the one problem with our happy-but-ever-expanding family was a severe lack of places for everyone to sit. Stanley had one armchair to himself (if you don't count the cat on his lap); Mum and Dad were sharing the other armchair; Rowan was on the beanbag, struggling to stretch her legs out 'cause of the three dogs flopped in front of the fireplace, while Linn and me were currently parked on the sofa, with Ivy on my lap and Grandma about to join us.

"And can I just say, Martin," Grandma chipped in, now that she'd helped herself to the last mug off the heaped tray she'd taken through from the kitchen, "*next* time you pull a disappearing act with your entire family, can you please leave me a note or a message on my answering machine so that I don't have a heart attack worrying about you all?"

Poor Grandma and Stanley; they'd meandered round to ours last night once they got back from their honeymoon, armed with shortbread biscuits and tales of sightseeing in Edinburgh, only to find the place as deserted as the *Mary Celeste* and Winslet happily shredding Tor's wellies, uninterrupted.

(By the way, I had to explain to Rowan that the *Mary Celeste* was an old ship that had been found floating with all the passengers mysteriously missing. She'd got confused, thinking it was the name of a women's magazine, and couldn't understand what Grandma was on about.)

After a momentary panic, our ever-sensible gran had gone next door and heard from Michael and Harry that we'd vamoosed to Cornwall, and slowly everything fell into place.

"Don't worry, Irene," Dad grinned. "I don't think there'll *be* a next time. I don't think anyone in this family will be doing any disappearing tricks ever again, will they?"

He aimed this last bit at Mum, who was sitting on the arm of his chair, looking very comfortable with Dad's arm wrapped protectively around her waist.

"You couldn't drag me out of this house with a herd of wild elephants!" Mum grinned back at him.

"Enough about elephants!" Grandma tutted amiably. "What about the practicalities?"

Before my parents could tell Grandma about Mum's friend Val offering to pack up Mum's flat and get her things sent here, and about their plans to buy a bunk bed so Ivy could share Tor's room (a plan Tor and Ivy were *delirious* about), the phone rang. And the millisecond the phone rang, Ben launched into an ear-splitting howl.

"Sorry!" Mum shouted above the din. "He always does his lone wolf impersonation when he hears a phone!"

She bent over and tried to clamp Ben's mouth shut, but it was too late; his new best buddies Rolf and Winslet looked sharply at him, decided it was an excellent game and set up their own lonesome howls.

Meanwhile, Tor darted through to answer the call, while Grandma winced at the racket and stared at her watch.

"Look what the time is already! We'd better get home and get Mushu fed!" she announced to Stanley, as she set her undrunk mug of tea back down on the table.

(Translation: "Look what a madhouse this is!

We'd better get out of here and leave them to it...")

"It's Alfie!" Tor roared above the baying.

Linn immediately made to get up, but sat abruptly down again when Tor yelled, "No – he wants to talk to Rowan!"

Poor Linn... It was going to take her a while to get her head around Alfie and Rowan, same as it was for me. But at least *I* wasn't shooting Rowan dirty looks as she scurried out of the living room...

In the flurry of Grandma and Stanley leaving, everyone, including our pet wolves and the odd cat, started milling around, giving cuddles and shouting byes and barking. Next thing, I found myself at the gate with Mum, holding Ben back as he enthusiastically tried to vault the wall and follow the nice man with the hairy ears who'd just been sneaking him bits of shortbread.

Once Grandma and Stanley were halfway down the street, me, Mum and a wriggling, bouncy Ben turned towards the house, and were met with a full-on view of total slushy-gushyness. There in the hall was Rowan, her head tilted girlishly, hugging the phone and talking into the receiver with a smile *so* wide it practically pinged right off the sides of her face. It would be obvious to anyone watching as far away as the spaceship *Endeavour* that they were witnessing true love.

"Hey," said Mum softly to me, as she patted Ben on the bum and sent him merrily scampering into the house. "It must hurt a lot when your own sister is going out with the boy you're crazy about..."

I went icy cold. Then boiling hot. Then icy cold again.

"How did you know?" I mumbled.

"It's just us mothers," Mum smiled, giving my hand a squeeze. "It's our job to know stuff."

My heart did a backward flip of happiness. All of a sudden, I knew I didn't have to be shy any more; Mum wasn't a stranger; she was my mum – who knew me better than anyone – and she was finally, *properly* home.

"Hope you like reading," I found myself smiling at her.

"Of course!" she nodded.

At last, it was time for her to pull up a chair and settle down with a cup of tea, a cat, and a huge pile of journals. After all, she had a serious amount of catching up to do...

Love (and happy reading, Mum!),

Ally ;c)

PS To help solve our seating shortage, Dad bought the world's worst sofa today from a second-hand shop in Stroud Green. It's swirly brown with bare patches, but Mum says she's going to buy some nice throws for it. Linn said the best throw for it would be to throw it in the skip down the street.

PPS I finally figured out the weird hoover dream! And it means (drum roll, please)... I don't fancy Alfie any more! I know – amazing, isn't it? The thing is, I had the hoover dream again last night, only this time round the attacking hoover turned into *Alfie* trying to give *me* a love bite. And when I woke up, I didn't need Rowan's dream book to work out that for me, romance sure *ain't* having to wear a Winnie-the-Pooh plaster on your neck all week to hide a bruise that's gone a yucky yellow colour. Love bites are so *blee*! How could Alfie do a blee thing like that?! Oh yes; it's official – I'm over Alfie. Well, OK, *semi*-over. (I'm not making any promises I can't keep...)

Out now:

Angels, Arguments and a Furry Merry Christmas

For the last two nights – since the Girls' Video Night round at Jen's – I'd had the strangest recurring dreams. They'd started the same way: I'd be all dressed up, waiting to go out on a date with Alfie. This wasn't so strange – I regularly dream daydreams and night-dreams about Alfie (dating him, holding hands with him, snogging the face off him), but the weird thing about these dreams was that I was dressed up as an angel, which wasn't too ideal if all we were going to do was go for a walk in the park or share a chicken nugget or three at KFC.

Then the dreams got *seriously* weird. In Wednesday night's version, Alfie turned up – all blond and cheekbones and irresistible as ever – and as we strolled out of the house (difficult with angel wings getting stuck in the doorway), he turned around to talk to me and had suddenly morphed into Keith Brownlow. Eeek!

If that wasn't weird enough, on Thursday night, I got to the same leaving-the-house point, and when Alfie turned around, this time he'd morphed into my boy buddy Billy, which was very, *very* blah indeed. I mean, the idea of going out on a date with Billy! I'd rather date Rolf – he's cuter...

Both nights, I woke up with a start, and had to put my bedside light on to calm down (which didn't go down well with the rudely awakened selection of pets that were sharing my room and bed, let me tell you).

"You look terrible," Sandie said, as she eyed me sympathetically at break-time today. "Are you OK, Ally?"

Nice one, Sandie, I thought to myself. *You score ten-out-of-ten for being a top-notch caring friend, but you'll have to do some homework if you want to get your grades up in the subject of Tact...*

"Just haven't been sleeping," I mumbled.

I probably *would* tell Sandie later what had been keeping me awake – she was coming back to mine for tea – but I didn't want to bring up my pathetic dating dreams in front of my other mates. Alfie fantasies aside, I'd just *hate* to come across as one of those wimpy girls who were always gagging to have a boyfriend or something. Why should I be? The only two of my friends who *had* dated didn't have exactly fantastic experiences. Salma went out with David Ling for four weeks and had about three private conversations with him in all that time, since every date seemed to include at least two of his mates tagging along like great big lemons. Then there was Jen; her boyfriend Gavin thought it was OK to mention casually which other girls he happened to fancy. Mmm, very flattering for Jen. *Not*...

"Oh, here comes Chloe now," said Kellie, pointing up the packed corridor as Chloe scurried towards us.

"Where have you been?" asked Jen. "You just vanished when we went to buy crisps!"

"Yeah – I just remembered that I should drop off that angel idea we had for the fashion show," Chloe replied, nicking a crisp out of Jen's open bag. "It was the closing day today, remember."

Um, no, I don't think any of us *had* remembered. It was pretty organized of Chloe to bother to write that suggestion out neatly and hand it in for us.

"So what's up with you today, Ally?" Chloe turned to me, with a mouth full of crisps. "You look terrible!"

"Well, thanks," I muttered sarcastically. "I just didn't sleep very well."

"No – I meant *that*!"

I glanced down where she was pointing and saw a gaping hole where the knee of my black, woolly tights should be.

"Rolf…" I growled, holding my leg out straight in front of me to examine the damage. You could practically *see* the teeth marks, where he'd chewed my knee when I was attempting to leave the house this morning. Because I'd woken up with a fringe that was pointing in all directions of the compass, I'd had to do some emergency blow-drying. Then I'd realized that both pairs of school trousers were in the wash, and had to stick on a stupid skirt, by which time I was so super-late that all I had time for was disengaging Rolf's teeth from my knee and I didn't bother to inspect the damage. I'd *wondered* why it was so breezy about the leg department when I was running to school…

"Is he still eating everything that isn't nailed down?" Salma grinned at me.

"Yep. Rowan came home with a bunch of pine cones she collected from Queen's Woods yesterday," I explained, letting Sandie and Jen take a turn at examining my knee. "She was going to spray them with leftover bike paint from Dad's shop – y'know, to make decorations – but she left them on the kitchen table for five minutes and when she came back, all she heard was the sound of Rolf crunching the last one."

It was odd, really. Winslet was the one who usually liked to chew or steal anything she could reach – which wasn't much, since her legs were so short her fuzzy belly practically skimmed the floor. Rolf tended to stick to eating dog food and any human food he could trick us out of. This current bad habit of trashing our house was making him the least popular pet at 28 Palace Heights Road, for sure. Well, except where Tor was concerned. He'd forgive an animal anything. A crocodile could bite Tor's arm off and he'd probably see the funny side.

"Why did Rolf attack your knee?"

"Did he break the skin?"

"No, he was just playing," I answered Sandie and Jen in one fell swoop, as I continued to stand on one leg, like a flamingo in school uniform. "He's never had much of a brain, but I don't know what's going on with him just now…"

I was staring hard at the ladder that was now gaping its way down from the ripped knee of my tights when I heard a Boy Someone say my name.

"Um, Ally…"

I turned around, slamming my foot down a little too hard in surprise. A few people close by visibly flinched at the loud *thwack* my black school shoe made on contact with the corridor's lino.

"Hello?" I mumbled uncertainly to Ben Something-Or-Other, as I racked my memory banks for his last name, and wondered in a panic what he could want with me.

"Um... I'm mates with Keith. Keith Brownlow. And he asked me to ask you..."

Instantly, the world slowed down all around me. I'm not a big-head, I'm not presumptuous, I couldn't actually *believe* this was happening to me when I'd spent the last few minutes talking about my mental dog while holding my leg in the air like a lunatic, but omigod – I was about to be asked out, if I wasn't wildly, madly, *insanely* deluded.

"...Keith was just wondering, like, if you..."

Ben Something-Or-Other had an awkward grin on his face, as if he'd taken on this job of messenger as a funny dare and was now finding it more embarrassing than he'd expected.

"...if you'd be up for going out with him. 'Cause he fancies you and everything."

Well, I'd *hope* it was 'cause he fancied me – if he wanted to go out with me because he *hated* me I'd have to *really* worry about his sanity and my safety.

It was only when I felt a tiny nudge in my back

from Sandie that I realized that I was now expected to say something in response. In a panic, I looked fleetingly around at my girlfriends for inspiration, but found only four stunned and grinning faces (Sandie, Jen, Kellie and Salma), and one stunned and *frosty* face (Chloe). What was all that about? Right now, the world had gone too weird to worry about a detail like that.

"Yes. OK. Fine. OK. Yeah, I would. Go out with him, I mean," I heard a voice witter dumbly. How *shamed* am I that it was mine.

"OK. Fine. I'll tell him," smirked Ben Something-Or-Other.

And he walked away, leaving me wondering what on earth was supposed to happen next, apart from my knees turning to pure custard and me crumbling to the floor in a fainting pile of panic.

"Help?" I muttered in the direction of my mates as soon as Ben Something-Or-Other wandered off.

Salma, Sandie and Kellie looked too stunned to say anything. Chloe looked too strangely grumpy to say anything. Luckily, Jen piped up with just the right thing.

"Crisp?"

"Thank you…" I said gratefully, helping myself to her packet.

Y'see, you might not know where you are with boys and emotions, but you always know where you are with salt and vinegar crisps...

There's always something going on in

ALLY'S WORLD

Make sure you keep up with the gossip!

(12)

VISITORS, VANISHINGS and va-va-va VOOM

Well, *zut alors* ... as if by magic, a whole bunch of very cute French boys has just turned up in Crouch End. (OK, so it's *not* by magic, it's 'cause of a school exchange trip. Oh, and there're girls too.) Me and most of mes *amies* are desperate to get close enough to torture them with our terrible French. All *mes amies* except Jen, that is – who's just pulled a vanishing act. *Uh-oh...*

Look out for loads more fab Ally's World books!
Find out more about Ally's World at

www.karenmccombie.com

brain full of plots, stupid stuff and cat hair

KMᶜC

the author

brain full of Pictures, football and cat hair

the illustrator